Curse & Spindle

A REALM OF REVELRY FAERIETALE

CHELSEY ANN TOMPKINS

For the ones who didn't want the pink or blue dress.
Obviously, make it purple.

Pronunciation Guide

Characters

Seraphine, SARA-FEEN
Phinie, FEE-KNEE
Korven, CORE-VEN
Fiola, FEE-OH-LUH
Urik, UR-ICK
Reshina, REH-SHE-NUH
Morella, MORE-EL-UH

Places

Riche REE-SH

Citrine Cliffs
REVELRY
Dunes of Ursharic

Brakish Wood
Moonstone Wood
Silver Isle
Heartstone Wood
Havenshire
Riche
Songbird Cove
CAT

CHAPTER 1

Korven

HER GOWN WAS ABSOLUTELY DEVASTATING.

And not in a good way.

White frills and lace for days on end wrapped snug around her stunning figure, encasing her body in a mass of fabric that acted as a cage. I had little doubt that's exactly what her wedding gown represented.

Seraphine Dupont's immaculate body deserved better than the layers upon layers of white brocade and delicate bows that shifted around her as she took her time walking down the aisle of the temple.

I had not spoken to her in fifteen years. She had become a woman in that time, no longer the girl with the golden locks who had read me stories beneath the sycamore trees when we'd both been children.

I cawed at the top of the rafter in my disgruntled state, rippling my feathers as a bad omen for what was to come.

After all, I was a bad omen for what was to come.

Seraphine's head, weighted in five-hundred marks worth of jewels, snapped in my direction. She had caught sight of me.

Good.

Color rose on her cheeks and her gaze narrowed. I gave another curt trill just to annoy her by showing up on the day of her nuptials to the great Prince Urik of Havenshire.

She, of course, could not know it was me perched atop the balustrade of the temple, though I'd imagine she was curious about the raven allowed in for the ceremony of the century.

Ignoring my third caw, she continued in her great pretense of happiness, about to marry the worst kind of man from what I had observed in the last week.

Not that I cared about their marriage outside of my plans to ruin it. She could have married anyone, and I'd be there the day of, flapping about, cawing at whatever other atrocious dress she donned.

The real reason for my presence was the curse.

Twenty-five years ago, a princess had been born on a night of a Cursed Moon. By the Veiled One's law, this meant that the little cherub would receive a curse, broken only by particular conditions.

Curse-giving was an unfortunate, yet orderly business, and handled by the Ravenfae Goddess Reshina who just so happened to be my mother. But Seraphine had been hidden away before Reshina could arrive to bestow the curse assigned to her.

Seraphine's parents, the King and Queen of Riche, hid her away and did so with greater success than you'd believe just by spending five minutes with them. They'd obviously had help from another of the fae Goddesses, but whom?

It didn't matter now. Curses could not be avoided, nor could they be broken before they were administered, and tonight, I would deliver this curse and be on my way.

I clicked my beak a few times more, twisting my black head to stare with my beady eye at the woman in white. Her violet eyes caught on me again. They'd grown to a deeper purple in the fifteen years since I'd looked into them and at that moment, teared ever so slightly as she continued her steps towards marriage.

Not that her emotional state mattered to me—I cared nothing for her.

Nothing whatsoever.

CHAPTER 2

Seraphine

WHY WAS A DAMNED RAVEN IN THE TEMPLE?

I swallowed thoughts of the bad omen and kept moving.

Twenty-two.

Twenty-three.

I knew it would take me precisely one-hundred and seventy-seven steps to reach Prince Urik of Havenshire. I had counted them the night before, practicing my gait towards shackles and the title of princess, which, if I made it through inevitable childbirth, would lead to the title of queen.

Goddess save me, I wanted to run.

Had I a choice, I'd have chucked my cascading bouquet of white lilies right in Urik's perfectly chiseled chin, turn on my heels, and bolt down the aisle to freedom.

Obviously, I had no choice.

None whatsoever.

My parents forced me here on this day, in this travesty of a wedding gown, which weighed me down and chafed my skin. All my life, I'd been happily living with the Forestfae, seeking nothing more than the pleasures of walking barefoot through the meadows, eating bramble berries directly from the vine, and rolling in the long grass with whichever handsome faerie sought the company of a human woman.

I had no desire to become a princess, to learn of my true heritage, or to join hands and sheets with this prick they called a prince.

I must be cursed, I thought to myself for the thousandth time, and the raven cawed again as if in agreement.

Fifty-five.

Fifty-six.

My hands itched to adjust the crown on my head, but that would be frowned upon. My fingers ached to pull at the over-sized satin bow across my chest, but that was hardly something the future Princess of Havenshire would do.

The last month of my life had been in preparation for this task to be handed off as no more than a bargain-priced princess—uncursed, unwed, most certainly not untouched, but there was nothing to do about that now.

When the King and Queen of Riche had traveled to Moon-stone Wood, arriving at my small cottage in the dead of night, I hadn't opened the door. After all, Fiola, Goddess of the Forestfae, wasn't keen on me speaking with people outside of her inner court, even if they did claim to be my long-lost parents. But when Fiola had shown up with them the next day, the royal carriage waiting, I had finally understood what this meant for me: shackles.

So there I was on step number eighty-nine with a Goddessdamn raven in the temple cackling alongside fate, for fate must have had a sense of humor to put me there. I didn't want to become the Princess of Havenshire. I did not want to bear the next line of kings—something I made sure I would not do anytime soon by taking the monthly tonic ahead of time.

Fate be damned, I enjoyed the life I had. I lived in my own

home and concocted my own jars of salves using the crystals grown in Moonstone Wood. I attended court of the Forestfae twice a month to give my devotion to their way of life and offer any new tinctures I had conjured from their lands. I had lovers, some friends, favorite clearings of soft grass and tall trees to shade me as I lie naked in the sun, soaking in the rays. I had plans to author books, dance with as many men—human or fae—I could find, and eat delicacies fed to me by such willing creatures.

I wanted to indulge, to seek pleasure, to please, to live.

I would do none of those things now.

I would be wed. Havenshire would finally have its matching princess to its handsome prince, and I would be paraded, and shown off as the long-lost Princess of Riche.

One-hundred.

One-hundred one.

Prince Urik's face became clearer as I neared. His pale blue eyes watched me with possession, with that royal pride that could fuck right off. I'd seen it in my own parents as they had explained my betrothal on the carriage ride to their castle in Riche. I'd been alone with him twice since then.

At first, I believed him to be quite handsome until he opened his arrogant, ugly mouth. He had boasted of lavish gowns and jewels commissioned for our tour of his kingdom after the wedding. He had draped a necklace around my throat, dripping with garnets, and pulled it tightly to choke me as he whispered in my ear, "Soon I will have you, and then that pretty little voice will sing for me alone."

One-hundred twenty-seven.

One-hundred twenty-eight.

I gulped, feeling the cold sweat slide down my back. What was really stopping me from running? How far could I reach in this gown before the guards hauled me back? What if I refused to participate? What if I fell to the floor, feigning illness so the wedding would be postponed? Maybe then I could find a way to escape. I couldn't go back to Moonstone Wood. Fiola had helped keep me hidden all my life, but had also promised to give me up when the time came.

If I married a prince, it would be difficult to deliver the curse I was destined to receive, for formal curse-giving would need approval from my husband, and my husband was to be the King of Havenshire. That meant protection. That meant a prison.

One-hundred fifty-two.

One-hundred fifty-three.

The orchestra weaving my song of chains to a man I did not love nor care to know seemed to grow louder, timed to my racing heart and the trailing sweat I felt everywhere in the bolts of fabric upon me.

My hands shook. One-hundred sixty-five, one-hundred sixty-six.

Urik held a well-manicured hand out to me as I reached the bottom steps of the altar. I halted, staring at the hand which held my future. The hand which was not my own.

The raven flew silently from its perch, soaring above us across the blue and violet stained glass windows depicting features of the fae Goddesses. I swallowed once again and looked into my betrothed's eyes. I took two more steps up to the altar and reached out my palm to place into his.

CHAPTER 3

Korven

SOARING FROM THE BALUSTRADE, I WATCHED HER reach for the prince. In a flash of acrid smoke and a few of my lesser coverts for show, I appeared on the steps below the altar in my fae form.

Gasps and a few well-timed screams rose from the pews, and I smiled at the woman I'd come to curse. "I regret to interrupt this happy occasion, but I have a little something for Princess Seraphine of Riche."

I tucked my feathered wings behind me, keeping my eyes on her as recognition flooded her face.

The prince grabbed her hand and yanked, ignoring her stumble, screaming, "Guards! Arrest him!"

"There's no need for that, Your Highness," I replied, pulling my drop spindle from my pocket. With a wave, the royal guards froze. Everyone in the temple benches froze. It was just myself, Seraphine, and her betrothed who could move or speak, and he was lucky I allowed such a courtesy.

"Now," I continued, balancing the spindle on one finger, spinning it like a top. Seraphine's eyes widened at the dark wood of the whorl etched with a pattern of dancing ravens that moved as it spun. "You, my dear, have avoided this curse long enough." I smirked, taking a step toward her. "It is time you take your dues."

"K-Korven?" she whispered, dropping her bouquet.

I hummed a laugh. "Phinie," I cooed, giving her a full smile.

"I will see you slaughtered for this, Ravenfae," Urik seethed.

"Ravenfae *Prince*," I corrected. "You know the laws of the Goddesses of the Veil as well as I. Your beloved princess was born under a Cursed Moon, and yet the curse was never delivered." I nodded toward her parents behind us, both frozen in rage. "You can thank your future in-laws for that."

"You...you're the one delivering the curse?" she stammered.

"Yes. Now be a good girl, Phinie darling, and prick your finger on the spindle."

Her violet eyes shifted back to the spindle growing darker in shadows as the whorl began to emit a low thrum. The pointed tip remained sharp and glinted, begging to be touched by a certain princess's finger.

"What will happen? What is my curse?"

I shrugged, ruffling my feathered wings a bit for dramatic flair. "It's not clear, even to Reshina. Your curse at birth was to prick your finger at sixteen years old and fall into a deep sleep that would cover your land and your people until the one who truly loved you kissed your lovely lips." I winked at the prince. "The curse has only grown since then. At twenty-five, who knows what the curse holds? Prick your finger on the spindle, and let's see what happens."

I took another step in her direction.

"This is preposterous!" Urik fumed. "I am her husband,

and I must receive formal documentation of this alleged curse! Return when you can provide the necessary—"

"Quiet." I waved the spinning spindle and his mouth clamped shut. He tore at his face with his fingers, a bottled scream coming from his chest.

"Phinie." I held the spindle out to her once more. "It grows stronger by the minute. You cannot escape your fate, darling girl."

Her eyes held mine with reckless abandon. I could not fathom whether she thought me her savior or her doom. Her lips parted and she drew a breath, taking her eyes from me and to the point of the spindle. With one last glance my way, she lifted her hand, raising her forefinger. As her skin broke on the sharp point, she mumbled under her breath, "If this kills me, I'm going to haunt you forever, Ravenfae Prince."

CHAPTER 4

Seraphine

DEATH WAS QUIET. DEATH WAS EASY. I DID NOT GO fighting—I went falling. The moment blood pooled along the tip of my finger, I felt the weight of it. I felt my eyes drifting to the back of my head. I began to fall, but someone caught me mid-air. It was the last thought I had before I slept the last dreamless sleep.

But someone was pulling. Someone was tugging, yanking. It felt as if my soul was parting from my chest, heaving me upright, disturbing my slip into an endless abyss.

I stumbled back, drifting a few steps down the altar steps.

No...I didn't.

I was there, sprawled across the altar as if a sacrifice in cascades of white to the Goddesses themselves. I blinked, frowning. Urik hovered over my body, holding my face upright, stroking my cheek in an unnaturally tender embrace.

"I should have guessed you'd be here." The rugged grumble came from Korven. He was staring at someone just over my shoulder.

I turned and gasped. "Fiola?"

She nodded, her rosy cheeks bobbing in excitement along

with the piled silver curls atop her head. "Yes, dearest, of course I'd be here. I knew he would come." She tsked. "You nasty raven, you. I admit, I expected Reshina herself to deliver this one. Is she preparing you to take over her duties? You have bad luck this time, meeting one of the Goddesses to alter the curse."

I gasped again. "You can alter the curse?"

"Of course, I can, sweet child!" she giggled. "I have done so already! Look down!"

I let my gaze fall to my feet. Only my feet were not there. Nor was my body. I could see the diamond pattern of the carpet through myself. I held my hands in front of my face, my mouth agape as I looked through my ethereal form to the benches of the temple, guests at my wedding still frozen from Korven's arrival.

"Am I dead?"

"Not entirely," Fiola responded flippantly. "Now, on to the next adjustments."

"It seems you have this handled," Korven began. "I've done my duty and will take my leave."

"You will stop right there, Korven, Ravenfae Prince of the Brackish Wood."

At her use of his full title, he froze, his black feathered wings unfurled as if he was moments from taking flight.

She cleared her throat. "That's better. Now, Seraphine, listen carefully." She stepped closer, reaching out as if to grab my shoulders as she had done many times back in her court in Moonstone Wood. "Oops," she laughed, her hands falling through my form. "Well, there is time to change that, dear. I could not reverse the curse. If I had not been sure to attend your wedding tonight, yes, you would be dead."

"Dead?" I whispered.

"Yes, dear, dead." She grinned, then shouted over my

shoulder, "Do stop that, Prince Urik! You're embarrassing yourself!"

I twisted to look at the altar where my betrothed pressed his lips to my lifeless body over and over, shaking me roughly.

"You cannot break the curse, you silly little man!"

"Who-who can?" I stammered.

She tittered, practically buzzing a foot below my gaze. "That's the fun of it, dear! We do not know!"

I shook my head, reaching up to pinch the bridge of my nose, only to find my hand drifting through my head.

She continued in glee. "Whether royal, baker, or candlestick maker, you must find the one who loves you most. Who loves you as you are, freckles, blush, and scars, at the next Cursed Moon, you must find the one who loves you most."

"Loves me most? What does that mean exactly?"

She laughed behind her hand. "I don't know that, either! That's the stipulation to break the curse. Now, I've been able to pull you from your body, so that you have the chance to find this person, but you only have until the next Cursed Moon to do it. This person must kiss *that* body's lips"—she pointed a periwinkle fingernail to the altar—"to break the curse. Only then will you fully return."

"Fully return?"

"Oh!" she squealed. "I don't want to spoil that! Now, you will need some assistance in this task as you are only visible to faekind, dear, and your curse breaker may not be fae at all! This is marvelous!" she exclaimed. "It will be so much fun to see how this ends."

She stepped around me, hands on her hips as she addressed Korven. "You will be helping her in this task."

"I will not," he responded, his lips moving but his teeth frozen shut.

"Don't take that tone with me, Prince. You have no choice in the matter, and Seraphine *needs* you."

His dark eyes pierced me as he took me in from top to bottom. I looked away, embarrassed to see him again after so many years. And as a ghostly figure, no less.

Fiola tapped his nose three times and his frozen body released. "There. Now your fate is bound to hers. If she dies, you die, so you'd better get a move on."

His wings spanned wide and he rolled his shoulders, cracking his neck. For a brief moment, he paused, taking me in again and then my body draped over Urik whose face seared with rage. Korven bent to meet Fiola head on. "If you've killed me, old woman, my mother will seek her revenge in blood."

"Oh, posh," she flicked his nose. "Your mother can't do a thing to me. And she must have known this was a possible outcome if she gave such a curse to one of my favorite humans. For all you know, she expected this very thing to happen."

His dark eyes darted to me again, and I straightened. My translucent body held no heart, but I felt as if I could hear it, pounding under his assessing gaze.

"Fine. Until the next Cursed Moon then. Do you have a suggestion on where we should start looking for this person?"

"Haven't the foggiest idea!" Fiola exclaimed, erupting in giggles again.

Korven sighed, spinning on his heels to approach the prince. "Keep her body in your castle. We will return in ten days with someone to kiss your betrothed."

Urik rose. "I will not stand for this! Bring her back!"

"Weren't you listening?" Korven scoffed. "To break the curse, she must be kissed by the one who loves her most." He cocked his head, the movement avian in nature. "Turns out, that's not you."

"If you think I'm going to let some beggar you find off the streets kiss my wife—"

In a flash of obsidian feathers, he lifted Urik by the puffed collar, holding him above his face. "She's not your wife," Korven seethed, "and you will allow anyone we bring back to kiss her because I'm not going to let us die from your idiocy. Understand, Your Highness?"

Urik gripped Korven's forearms, nodding. The Ravenfae let him go, turned and walked down the aisle. "Let's go, Princess."

"Is she really there?" Urik called, his eyes darting all around.

I lifted my hand to wave wildly at him. "He truly cannot see me. Can he hear me?"

Korven stopped at my side and leaned in closer. "Not sure —want to say how you really feel?"

I laughed abruptly. "Urik, you absolute *shit*, I hate you and will never marry you! Do not touch my body, do not even look at me, you pompous ass!"

I drew a sharp breath, surprised at my own outburst. Urik did nothing but continue his deep-set frown, his pale eyes darting all over the temple for any sign of me.

Fiola giggled in her way. "Go now, you two. I'll finish up here and explain. Time is ticking." She tapped her hip as if she wore a pocket watch.

"You heard her, Phinie." Korven whispered low into my ear. "Let's fly."

CHAPTER 5

Korven

SERAPHINE WAS A NATURAL. IN HER ETHEREAL FORM, she lifted to the sky, rising above the tops of the temple towers. Though her body was light like gossamer silk, she still wore that ridiculous dress. It floated around her as she beamed up at the stars, arms outstretched, reaching for the few wafts of clouds in the night sky.

I shifted, donning my raven form and flying across the tops of the trees with her.

Her laughter was beautiful.

Considering she'd been dead minutes ago, the sound that drifted in the night was carefree and wild.

I'd heard it before, but that was a long time ago. We were different now, no longer children playing underneath an old tree.

"This is incredible!" she called to no one in particular.

I cawed in reply, flying through the bottom of her dress just to experience what it felt like. She shrieked and began to fall. I dove underneath her form, guiding her back up to the sky. I doubted she could actually be hurt, but she'd been through enough, and I needed her sane so we could end this Goddessdamned curse and move on with our lives.

She floated above the trees outside of the temple, her ghostly hand over her chest. "So," she began, "You and I will...that is, both of us need to—"

I flapped my wings, cawing once more before soaring towards town. I circled back, asking her to follow.

As we neared the main streets, our destination loomed tall in the thin moonlight. The Rose and Briar was a seedy place. The few rooms of the inn above the tavern were small, worn, and easy to slip in and out of—perfect for a Ravenfae Prince waiting for a lost princess to show up for her wedding. The smoke rising from the chimney stack smelled of roasted mutton and freshly baked bread, reminding me that I had meant to deliver the curse and leave in time to eat dinner— perhaps even pick up a companion downstairs for the night.

I'd picked one up all right. Only she was a cursed princess, visible only to faekind, fly-through, and see-through.

I circled the building and landed on the window ledge of the top floor room. I had left it open for myself in case I needed a quick escape back. I pecked the window open a little more and flew inside, shifting immediately and pulling at the window frame to allow Seraphine through, even though she didn't need me to.

She floated into the room in an easy step down from the ledge as if she'd done it a hundred times.

"That's better," I said, closing the window and lighting the lanterns. "Now, let's discuss our strategy for finding the one who loves you most. This is my room at the top of the Rose and Briar Inn. We are in the town of Thornhill in the Kingdom of Havenshire."

"How did you know I was about to ask?"

I shrugged, folding my arms across my chest. "It'd be the first thing I'd want to know if I were you."

She fiddled with her hands, awkwardly trying to fold them before her, instead swiping them through her own body. Sighing, she glanced around the room. "Look, I know this is strange—"

"We're past strange, Phinie. This is fate."

Her face fell. "You remember, then? The name you used to call me?"

My black wings flared slightly behind me, always revealing my inner thoughts. "It was a long time ago."

Nodding, she began to pace in soundless footfalls. "Right. We don't have to talk about the stupid games we played as children. I'm sorry you're now bound to my fate, but you kind of deserved it crashing in on my wedding and cursing me to death."

"I was only doing the task given to me by a Goddess."

"But on the night of my wedding, Korven?"

"Don't tell me you were looking forward to its completion."

"I wasn't! But I didn't want—" She stopped, turning to me in frustration. "I never wanted to marry Urik, but I didn't want to die, either."

"Glad that's out of the way."

"What I'm trying to say is, thank you for interrupting, but fuck you for killing me."

My chest shook in laughter. "You're welcome. Now, you gather your thoughts and questions. I'm going to get something to eat downstairs. I'll be back in an hour."

I pushed off the window, headed for the door.

"You're leaving me here alone?" she squeaked, reaching out a hand to grab my arm. She couldn't.

I raised a brow. "Are you frightened to be alone?"

A visible gulp raced down her throat. I tracked the movement.

"Not usually."

Opening the door, I gestured for her to leave first. "Faekind don't often visit the town of Thornhill. It's unlikely anyone will be able to see or interact with you. Except me."

"Sounds like a better night than I expected," she laughed nervously.

I chuckled. "Agreed."

CHAPTER 6

Seraphine

I'D NEVER BEEN INSIDE A TAVERN. THE JAUNTY FIDDLE striking chords among the voices, the sound of flagons of ale clopping down onto stained, sticky wooden tables, the shouts of arguments—all of it was overwhelming. I was thankful I could not be seen.

Korven leaned in to ask, "First time?"

I nodded in reply, closing my mouth which had hung agape watching a barmaid with her tongue down the throat of a man whose hands were covered in tattoos.

"Follow me," Korven said, catching the eye of a barmaid rushing three mugs of ale to another table. He pointed over the crowd to a tall, more intimate booth at the back of the tavern and she nodded, apparently knowing his order already.

He slid into the seat of the old wood and gestured for me to do the same.

I twisted my lips. I hadn't really walked down the stairs. Nor had I walked across the floor of the Rose and Briar. I had done more of a glide and felt myself pass through plenty of rowdy patrons.

I focused on my movement and attempted to slide into the

seat opposite, instead falling straight through the wooden bench, finding myself upside down looking into the cellar of the place. I heard his laughter all the way from the floor below, booming through the jovial banter of the bar's drunkards. I let myself hang upside down for a moment, my feet somewhere still up above. I gave a great sigh and concentrated.

I rose through the floor, focusing well enough to sit in a position across from the Ravenfae Prince. He watched me appear, tearing off a chunk of crusty bread and dipping it into a meaty stew.

"That was fast," I remarked.

"The food or you relearning how to sit?"

I gave him a frown.

"Don't look at me like that, Princess. You've only got a few days of this, and you'll be back to your gorgeous self or we'll both be dead."

I wondered if he could see my cheeks flush.

"So," he drawled, "any ideas on where we should start looking for this beau of yours? Got any lovers? Any admirers? General onlookers?" He took a swig of ale. "I'm sure you've got plenty of those."

"Yes and no," I replied, watching a group of men gather onto a table and begin to sing off-key. "I've had lovers. No one who could break this curse, though."

"So you've never been in love?"

"No," I lied quickly.

His dark eyes narrowed. A waft of hair fell into his face, so black it had a blue sheen. "I find that difficult to believe."

"Why?"

"I remember you laughing, Phinie." He wiped his mouth and sat back, folding his arms while his black wings splayed behind him. "A laugh like that doesn't go unnoticed for long. There had to be someone who heard it and fell at your feet."

I slowly shook my head. "No one," I whispered.

His gaze sharpened again. Through his straight dark brows and down his long nose, he watched my face for any sign of falsehood.

My heart beat swiftly under his unwavering scrutiny.

He finally cleared his throat and pushed his food aside, leaning on the table. "We have a lot of searching to do then, Princess."

"Who *are* you talking to?" A red haired, buxom woman slid into my bench. I hurriedly scooted over so she wasn't sitting unknowingly through my lap.

Korven's face broke into a roguish grin. "Myria. This night keeps getting better."

The woman beamed, flicking her long curled locks behind her shoulder, leaving her creamy freckled skin exposed. "My favorite Ravenfae Prince. I figured you'd be long gone by now...considering."

Korven quirked a brow. "Considering?"

Myria swiped his mug, taking a long gulp that dribbled slightly down her chin and to her breasts. Without missing a beat, she grinned, pulling her fingers along her skin and sucking the ale off each one. "Considering not one hour ago a Ravenfae Prince showed up to ruin the wedding of Prince Urik."

"News travels fast around here."

"Just about everything is fast around here, Korven." She paused for her meaning to settle.

I took a deep breath, debating whether I should launch myself into the floorboards and die again, this time of embarrassment.

As if sensing my discomfort, he glanced at me quickly

with a slight shake of his head. "Well, Myria, I find myself staying in the area longer than I had planned. Curse business."

"How delightful," she cooed. "Any business I could help you with?"

Her meaning was unmistakable. I cleared my throat, rising to leave them to whatever tension they needed to release.

Korven dusted his hands over the table and rose as well. "Actually, I believe there is. I'm looking for eligible bachelors. And I'm starting my inquiry here in Thornhill. Do you know of any gentlemen's clubs where I might speak to the owner?"

"Bachelors?" she shrieked, rising as well. "Whatever for?"

He shook his head, wings rustling. "Curse business, remember?"

She pouted in a huff. "I was hoping to help you in a... different manner tonight." She stepped closer to him, her chest meeting his in an intimacy I knew was formed before this night.

"I appreciate your offer, but I'm here strictly on work business."

Her pout deepened and she backed away. "Sounds like you could use a little break, Prince."

I spoke up before I could stop myself. "I can go, Korven. It's your room and it's not like I'm going to need to sleep anytime soon anyway. I can meet you down here in the morning."

His eyes turned to me still standing awkwardly inside the booth, half of my body through the wood. He kept his gaze on mine, answering Myria. "As I said, I'm here for work, and that's all. If you wish to help, kindly give me the name of Thornhill's gentleman club."

Myria scoffed. "You assume I'd know."

Korven looked her up and down, silently crossing his arms at his chest in wait.

The woman visibly melted and I understood why. Korven, Ravenfae Prince of the Brackish Wood, was—simply put—gorgeous. Easily the tallest man in the room, he stood with a lean grace of muscled arms that pulled his black shirt tight in the movement. He wore black leather pants with a few small daggers hooked at the sides and ankle black boots. The black of his attire, wings, and hair only drew my eyes to the golden undertones of his skin.

"Alright, fine," she conceded. "But I expect a favor in return someday. I know a place, and I know the owner. He can help you with your...inquiry."

Korven nodded his agreement.

"The mansion is located a mile from here to the east. The sign out front says *The Forest and Friends* but no one calls it that."

"Oh, really?" Korven asked in a chuckle.

"Really. Anyone who's anyone uses another name. The Burrow."

CHAPTER 7

Korven

"IT'S ALRIGHT, YOU KNOW," SERAPHINE STARTED WHEN we arrived back in my room. "I can stay downstairs if you…if you and her—"

"You said you don't want to be alone, remember?" I looked up at her floating near the stack of books I'd been reading in my week of waiting for her wedding night. I unlaced one of my boots, tossing it to the side of the bed before beginning with the other.

She heaved a heavy sigh, tilting her head to read the spines in the pile. "I meant I didn't want to be alone right then. I–I'm used to this form now."

I gave her a doubting look and rested my arms across my legs.

"Well," she continued with a little laugh, "I'm at least more used to it."

"I've tangled myself into Myria's web before. Almost didn't make it out last time. Fool me twice, right?"

"Oh," she mumbled, twirling around to face away from me as I unbuttoned my shirt.

I continued to undress, keeping my pants on for her sake

and slipped into my bed, the old wood groaning through the room. I folded my arms at the back of my head, adding, "Nothing serious."

"It's fine," she assured quickly. "I don't have to be privy to details of your love life."

"Speaking of, let's talk about what kind of man you want to fall for you in the next few days."

She moved to rub her eyes, giving up and sitting on a small chair at the rickety table instead. "Well, I guess someone kind."

"Done. What else?"

"Someone quiet, but...clever. Someone I'd want to read books with by the fireplace, but we wouldn't need to talk... we'd just...be silently happy together."

"A cleverly quiet, kind reader," I mused. "Might be difficult to come by in this town, Princess, but we're sure as Goddessdamned gonna try."

"I don't want you to do that," she huffed.

"Do what?"

"Call me 'Princess'. I'd rather not be, and I don't want to be reminded I am...that."

"Done," I sighed, shutting my eyes and settling into the quiet.

But the stillness irked me. Even through the typical ruckus humming from below, I couldn't help but wonder what she would be thinking through the night. She wouldn't need to sleep—probably couldn't in this state. I peeked an eye open to watch her. She had her legs pulled up so that her ghostly chin looked as if it rested on her knees. Goddess, her dress was ugly. It splayed around her legs and trailed to the floor in gobs of fabric, drowning her, letting her fall away to obscurity.

Irritated, I recognized that I'd get no sleep like this. I rose from the bed, lighting the few candles in the room.

Her eyes, an iridescent violet in this form, locked onto my torso. I chuckled to myself, sure to flex a little for her benefit...and mine.

Silently, I pulled the books from the table into my arms, opening each one to the first page. I dug into my pocket for rocks, weighing down the cover of each as I placed them open on the floor. Then, still in that easy silence, I pulled a book of Revelry maps from my satchel, spreading its edges across the floor and settling a heavy stone on each corner.

"There. Something for you to read and study while I catch some sleep. It won't be long. I can't sleep more than a few hours at a time."

She looked on in disbelief. "You...you keep rocks in your pockets?"

I gave a chuckle, nodding. "Raven, remember?"

A visible shiver racked through her body as she stood, eying everything displayed on the wooden floor. "Thank you," she said.

"You're welcome. Now study up tonight." I pointed to the unfolded map. "I'll have some follow-up questions to ask you about Revelry in the morning."

I fell back into the bed, this time facing the window away from her. Phinie needed something to distract her from what the curse had done. And I needed to know I hadn't royally fucked up her entire existence.

CHAPTER 8

Seraphine

KORVEN STIRRED AWAKE A FEW HOURS BEFORE DAWN. I'd tried not to watch the tiny clock near his bed, waiting for him to wake and question me about what he'd left me to read and study. Since he had displayed his treasures, at least an hour of my time had been to steady my nerves of what the morning would bring. Another hour to actually read and look over the map. The last hour to crush any of the strange familiarity I had felt being in his presence again.

It was fifteen years ago that we had first met under that old sycamore tree at the edge of the Moonstone and Brackish Woods. Our lives had changed much since then. We both had futures to live and the fact that my curse had brought us back together didn't actually matter. It was a coincidence that he was the one to deliver my curse and that Fiola decided to tie my life to his. Nothing about this was divine or meant to be in any way.

Nothing whatsoever.

"Morning, Phinie darling." His raspy voice would have heated my blood if I'd had it pumping through my ethereal form. He sat up in the bed, spreading his wings wide in a long stretch.

"Good morning!" I said, cheerier than I felt.

He flicked a hand back through his hair, exposing his widow's peak and dragged the sleep from his eyes. "How did the reading go?"

"I-I read everything and I think I've got Revelry down."

He reached into his satchel and took a long drink from his waterskin. Wiping his mouth with the back of his hand, he gestured to the floor where all of his books were still open to the first page. "And which book intrigued you most?"

I floated over to my favorite so far. "This one."

He nodded, reaching for his shirt, fitting it through special cutouts for his wings. "It's got romance, you know."

"I can tell."

"I'll turn the pages for you before I go."

"Go?"

"I've got some people to speak to before we get started today. I have an idea on how we can set this up, but I'm going to need some cooperation from the right people." He slid his feet into his boots and laced them quickly.

As he stepped around the small room, flipping each page, I asked, "By cooperation, do you mean forcing by magic?"

He chuckled, turning the last book and reconfiguring the small shiny pebbles holding it open. "Ravenfae magic is a bit unpredictable at times. But since these tasks are curse business, I should be able to use my more...persuasive magic easily enough to get what we need."

"Should...should I come, too?" I added, doing what I could to keep the unease from my voice.

He rose from bent knees to face me near the window. "Well, I would invite you along since the outcome of this curse dictates your life as much as mine, but I think it's best we keep you like this—hidden as much as possible. I don't know if there are any faekind at the Burrow, and it's best I find out without you. I expect to be back in an hour at dawn, if that was your next question."

I gave him a small smile. "It was."

His dark brown eyes lowered to the top of my dress. I looked down, my mouth twisting at the enormous satin bow draped across my ghostly chest. His eyes lifted back to my face, and I took a breath to tell him I had no part in choosing such an awful wedding gown.

But before I could speak, he shifted, soaring through the open window and into the night air. I watched him disappear across the dark sky, half a moon illuminating his silky feathers. Feathers I had known once. Feathers that had curled around me as I had drifted to sleep under an old tree whose roots stretched across the lands of both of our homes.

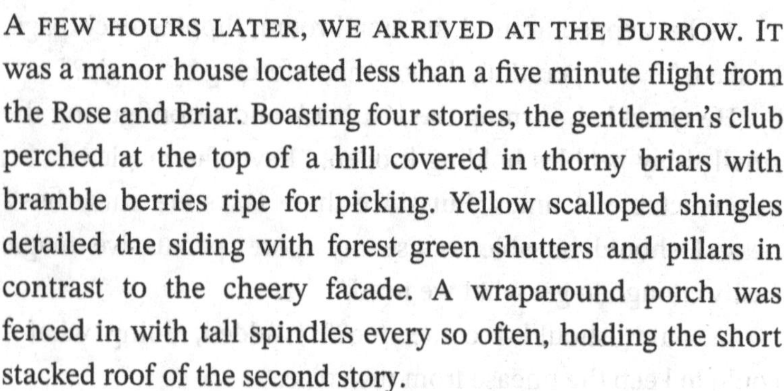

A FEW HOURS LATER, WE ARRIVED AT THE BURROW. IT was a manor house located less than a five minute flight from the Rose and Briar. Boasting four stories, the gentlemen's club perched at the top of a hill covered in thorny briars with bramble berries ripe for picking. Yellow scalloped shingles detailed the siding with forest green shutters and pillars in contrast to the cheery facade. A wraparound porch was fenced in with tall spindles every so often, holding the short stacked roof of the second story.

I floated next to Korven on the ground, my head leaning back to view the fourth floor, which was nothing more than one room in the tallest tower of the manor house. An enormous clock ticked in the early hours of morning above the window.

"What exactly do gentlemen…do at the Burrow?" I asked, admiring the overhangs of carved scrollwork across the third story balcony.

Korven glanced sideways at me, a grin blooming across his sharp features. "All gentlemanly things, I'm sure."

I squinted back at the mansion, doubting that entirely.

He sighed and continued. "Kind things, clever and quiet things." He shrugged. "I'd bet two hundred marks there's even a library inside. All we need to do now is find the reader." He continued forward, headed up the first steps, "Might be difficult to find, however. Seeing as he'll be quiet and all."

"Are you teasing me about my ideal man?" I asked, unable to keep the amusement from my voice.

His wings shifted and he turned his head over his shoulder. "I would never, Phinie darling."

Before I could reply, he rapped on the dark green door three times. I hurried up the steps after him, just in time to see a squat man open it. He bowed low. "Your Highness, we were expecting you. Right this way." He gestured inside and I followed close behind, floating through Korven's wings slightly to avoid the closing door.

The man couldn't see me, obviously not faekind, and addressed Korven again. "The Hare is waiting for your arrival on the fourth floor. Please follow this staircase and he will greet you there before you begin your inquiry."

Korven nodded, thanking the man and beginning up the winding stairs to the left of the foyer. I followed, holding my questions, instead taking in every feature of the manor. Just as detailed as the outside, the rooms promised a wealthy clientele. Oil painted portraits of men in varying ages lined the walls. We passed the door to a sitting room, pipe smoke lingering in the air over chartreuse velvet couches. I wanted to float through the walls, exploring further, but Korven's heavy footfall on the winding stair brought me back to our task at hand. We reached the top of the tower and Korven knocked on the single scarlet red door, which clashed with the rest of the club's decor.

The door swung open on iron hinges and a portly man held his arms wide, greeting Korven like an old friend. "Prince Korven! Just in time, good sir! I've completed the names of suitors not five minutes past. Forty-two today, but word has not reached all of the Burrow's patrons quite yet, I assure you."

Korven nodded, stepping into the room. Again, I shifted through just in time to avoid the door that would swing through me anyway if I missed my opening. A bay window sat across the room with brilliant crimson curtains pulled back on hooks, showcasing a perfect seat for reading a good book. A long desk of dark cherry wood was the only furniture in the room besides two maroon high backed chairs.

"Will a guest be joining you?" the man I assumed was the Hare asked, gesturing to the seats as Korven pulled out the first and then the second.

"Soon, I hope. We'll see," he said, sliding into one chair and adjusting his wings in the movement. He picked up the scroll of parchment, holding it close to his face. The Hare shifted on his feet with a subtle unease.

The man cleared his throat as Korven ignored his presence. "Well, I'll leave you to it, Your Highness. The first batch of bachelors will arrive at a quarter past. Please do call down to a Cardinal if you need assistance or anything at all." He moved to the bell pull near the door. "One tug and a Cardinal will be with you within the minute."

Korven lowered the scroll slightly, staring across the room

at the Hare. The man took it as the dismissal it was and quickly left, closing the door behind him.

The moment he was gone, Korven reached into his tunic, pulling a pair of black-rimmed spectacles from an inside pocket and placing them across his face.

"Come here," he grumbled.

I did as he said, unsure if I was more in awe that he wore reading glasses or that he had orchestrated this entire ordeal in the early hours of a single morning. I hovered in the chair he had pulled for me and placed my hands in my lap, leaning closer to take a look at the list of names on the scroll of parchment.

The names meant nothing to me. It was a simple list of gentlemen who I assumed Korven planned to meet and interview for potential curse breakers.

"You planned all of this in the mere two hours since dawn?" I muttered under my breath, pausing at the name Sir Fredrix Gorthenshire of Fredrixshire. Each name was more ridiculous than the last.

"I can be very convincing, Phinie darling. You once knew that."

I blushed, remembering his reference. "So these men are arriving today and then what? You ask them about their reading habits?"

He continued to read the names down the list, marking a few with the quill left for him on the table. "Would you rather I start inquiring to men on the streets?"

I sighed, resigned to this idea of his—the best we had so far. "No." I tapped my foot against the floor, meeting no resistance from the wood as my satin slipper fell through. "Please just...send them away if I ask. If any of these men are anything like Urik, I doubt we'll be going in the right direction. And their names..." I trailed, leaning closer again to read another: Count Tristan Delacroix le Cul of Swepton.

"Done," he muttered, sliding the glasses off his nose and back into his inner pocket. "I will shoo away any bachelor not to your liking for any reason whatsoever. Down to too many hairs in his nose."

I laughed, relaxing a bit and rolling my shoulders. "Alright, Your Highness," I mocked, reaching out as if to elbow him in the arm. "Let's find a curse breaker."

CHAPTER 9

Korven

"AND WHAT WAS THE LAST BOOK YOU READ, DUKE Broughford?" My quill was ready, poised above the imbecile's name. One more idiotic thing from his mouth, and he'd be gone from the scroll and out the door.

"M-my last book?" A bead of sweat broke down his forehead and he reached into the pocket of his burgundy vest, pulling a handkerchief monogrammed with an enormous B embroidered in delicate flowers. One his mother likely sewed for him. "I-I don't remember the title, Prince Korven, but...but the subject was"—he cleared his throat and wiped his forehead—"hunting. Yes, yes, it was a book about hunting pheasants."

I took a sidelong glance at Seraphine beside me. Her arms were folded at her chest and her feet tapped in irritation, falling through the floor of the tower room continuously. Her adorable little nose scrunched upwards while her lips pulled into a clear frown. She wasn't impressed and neither was I.

"Are you telling me, Duke Broughford," I began, "that the last book you read was about killing birds?" I shifted my wings, reminding him of what I was.

"N-no! I swear it was just a book I looked through! I-I didn't even really read any of the words—just looked at the pictures!"

I hid a chuckle. "So, you're telling me the last book you read was a picture book, Duke Broughford?"

"It wasn't—I was—"

"I've heard enough." I scratched his name off the scroll. "You are excused."

The man looked relieved and as he turned to open the door, Seraphine exhaled, her shoulders relaxing slightly.

"He was worse than the last," she mumbled, lifting her hands to her face. "Who *are* these men?"

"Bachelors of the Burrow, darling." I sighed myself and then laughed, remembering how Sir Bristleshaft did not like my joke about his name.

She leaned towards me, looking over the list. "How many are left?"

"Three. Then we'll be free until the Hare can give us more tomorrow."

She sighed heavily. "I'm not sure this is going to work." Her eyes narrowed at the crimson door with more men waiting just outside for their turn to enter.

"We had to start somewhere. And I don't trust Urik to solve this problem." I paused for a moment, carefully watching her reaction to my next words. "Fiola said he must be the one who loves you most. She didn't say you have to love him back."

She turned to face me instantly. "What are you saying? I should be focused on who I think could love me and less on whom I could love?"

My wings ruffled of their own accord. "Perhaps."

She shifted back to stare at the bright red door. "Who

could love me most..." She gave a nod. "Alright. Bring the next one in."

I stood and stretched, flaring my wings wide and reaching my arms up over my head. She stared up at me with those violet eyes of hers and smiled softly.

I felt the side of my mouth tilt upwards, but it didn't matter what her eyes said or what summersaults my heart did as she watched me. She had three more gentlemen to meet, and I had a curse to help her break.

CHAPTER 10

Seraphine

"ASK HIM IF HE'S BEEN TO MOONSTONE WOOD," I whispered, even though Lord Yevin of Halishcourt couldn't hear me.

Korven placed his quill on the desk, almost ready to cross out this man's name along with the last forty-something of them. But this was our last chance for the day and the sun was making it well known, sharing her rays of orange light across this gentleman's face from the window behind us.

Lord Yevin squinted, shielding his eyes with his hand as Korven asked, "Have your travels led you to Moonstone Wood, Lord Yevin?"

Tall and handsome, the man with blonde hair swept to the side smiled. "I've not had the pleasure, Prince Korven. I believe that Moonstone Wood borders your home, does it not?"

"Indeed," Korven murmured. "And what interests do you seek to share in a future partner, Lord Yevin?"

"I've been thinking about this," the Lord replied.

I perked up, listening carefully. I stilled my foot—the same one I'd been tapping all day through the floor in irritation.

"Go on," Korven replied, leaning forward on the desk and clasping his hands in front of his chest.

"We were not given an exact reason for this interview, you see," Lord Yevin replied, stepping closer. "The Hare sent word that a member of a royal house was looking for a life partner. More than that, this person was seeking someone to love them." He stepped closer still, a mere two steps from the desk.

He had a chiseled face with a square chin and soft gray eyes. His gaze lit in what I could only describe as a smolder as he leaned in above Korven and said softly, "You are royalty, are you not, Ravenfae of the Brackish Wood?" He hummed, parting his lips softly. "I am the last bachelor here. And lucky for you, Prince, I do not seek a woman in a life partner."

Shocked at his assumption, I made the movement of biting my lips together, my eyes wide on Korven.

The Ravenfae Prince didn't flinch. His dark eyes didn't leave the Lord's face, who only took that as encouragement.

"I believe I might be just what you are looking for," the gentleman spoke low, now leaning on the desk with both hands.

Korven cocked his head and leaned forward. "Unfortunately for everyone in this room, you are not. Thank you for your time, Lord Yevin. You may go."

The Lord stood upright. "I apologize, Your Highness. I didn't mean to imply—"

"There is no need," Korven said dismissively, waving him off with one hand and crossing out Lord Yevin's name with the other.

"If I came across as something other than I am, I would prefer you—" the Lord started again.

"Lord Yevin," Korven bit back in annoyance. "It has been a long day. You are tired. Whatever you have just said will not leave this room, nor is it a concern of mine for whom you wish to spend your life with." He stood and stared him down, an impressive few inches taller. "You have my word. I wish you well."

The Lord of Halishcourt nodded once and left. I sighed, crossing my arms and tapping my foot again.

"Goddess, save us," he sighed with me, walking around the table to pace by the door. "What fresh hell is this? Another week and I'll die, even if we do find someone to kiss your lips in time." He rubbed his face and I looked over the list once again.

"You should get some rest," I replied in a huff, irritation just as evident in my voice. "We can only hope that lot was the worst of them. Perhaps the most desperate? Lord Yevin said they knew about the royalty part of it. These might be the men most likely to respond in hopes of becoming part of a royal family." I scoffed loudly. "The joke's on them. I'm no more of a princess than Myria. And she knows more of the men who frequent this place than I do." I groaned. "Goddess knows I could never see any of these men loving me."

"What is that tapping sound?" he asked, looking around the room.

I stopped my train of thought, listening with him. "I don't hear anything," I confirmed after a moment.

He looked my way, his mouth lifting into a grin.

"What?" I asked, bemused. "What are you—"

He strode towards me, pulling the desk away from the chairs where I still sat. "What—"

"Look down."

I did just as he said. There, below my illusory gown, were two white slippers on my feet, solid on the hardwood floor.

CHAPTER 11

Korven

"MAY I?" I ASKED, SLIDING TO MY KNEES BEFORE Seraphine.

Wide-eyed, she gulped and nodded.

I slid my hand behind her ankle, lifting her foot to my thigh. "Fascinating," I murmured.

"I'd say bizarre," she replied. "Why have my feet returned to solid flesh? And what about the rest of me?"

I slipped her shoe from her foot, letting it clatter to the ground as I lifted her ankle further so she could see it. She wiggled her toes. "Phinie darling, I'd say this means we're on the right track."

WALKING BACK TO THE ROSE AND BRIAR, WE discussed what her body returning meant.

"Do you think one of those men was the right one for me? Or that we must be closer to finding him?" She walked beside me, just her feet and ankles visible to anyone who might be looking. That was another problem to solve; how would we explain as parts of her began to solidify?

"I would guess the latter, considering your repulsion for each gentleman we came across today. Though, if there are any of the forty-two you'd like to invite back—"

"No!" she all but shouted. "No, there wasn't a single one of them I'd ever like to see again."

"Done," I confirmed. "We'll arrive tomorrow and find new names ready to be interviewed."

"And..." she trailed, stopping for a moment at a ripe patch of bramble berries. "How will we hide my feet? I can't just sit there again with white slippers on the floor and nothing of the rest of me."

"A blanket over your chair down to the floor should—"

"Would you eat one of these for me?" she interrupted.

I stopped, backtracking to where she pointed. A rather prickly vine bent heavily with seven bramble berries—purple, plump, and ripe for any passerby to pick. "You'd like me to eat a berry?"

She shrugged shyly. "They're my favorite. If I can't have one, I want you to."

I pondered for a moment what it might be like to share a handful of ripe, succulent berries with Seraphine Dupont. Banishing the thought from my mind, I plucked one of the darkest berries, popping it into my mouth and chewing slowly.

Her breath hitched in a clear sound and she watched my mouth in what I'd describe as nothing short of...hunger.

"Good?" she whispered.

I licked the side of my mouth, something stirring within me as she tracked my tongue. "Delicious," I replied, pulling three more and tossing them into my mouth.

We continued on down the hill. She stayed close to my side, careful to not be trampled by the people of Thornhill darting through the streets.

The Rose and Briar stood tall a few streets away and she spoke up. "I'll leave you to your night. That is, if you don't mind escorting my feet back to ou—your room."

"Can't do it," I replied, nudging her now muddy slipper towards one of the many food stalls along the market road. "I've met enough strangers today. Looking forward to a quiet dinner with an old childhood friend." I smirked when she frowned. I paid for my roll of bread, nuts, dried meat, and cheese.

"Old childhood friend?" she asked on our way back into the inn.

"What else would you call what we were?" I opened the door for her, staying close to her feet as we headed up the stairs. The downstairs tavern was only half-full. I had no doubts it'd be overflowing in a few more hours.

"I'd say we were...strangers who met one day under a sycamore tree."

"Strangers..." I wondered at her use of the word, unlocking our room and pushing the door open to allow her to step inside.

"I mean," she continued, slipping out of her muddy shoes and stepping towards the meager fireplace. "We were barely ten years old." She shrugged. "Strangers."

I had fond memories of those few weeks we'd spent together as carefree children. I'd never call us strangers. "We are more strangers now than we were back then." I set my dinner on the small table, pulling a knife from my belt and slicing the bread in half, making a sandwich of sorts with the meat and cheese.

"Would...would you mind lighting a fire? My feet are cold."

"Done," I said through a mouthful of food. I lit the fire and left her to warm her toes, finishing my dinner quickly before changing out of my tunic and into a softer black shirt that fit my wings better. Seraphine sat silently before the fireplace the entire fifteen minutes. Her toes wiggled before the flames and she wrapped her ghostly arms around her ethereal knees.

I kept the silence, too. We didn't need to speak. We'd heard enough speaking for the day in meeting so many men who, honest-to-goodness, were not worth Seraphine's time. Nor mine.

I flipped each page of the books still open across the floor and stood beside her, holding out my fingers to warm them at the fire. "Can I sit with you, Seraphine?"

She looked up from the dance of flames, her mouth opening slightly in the movement, her eyes big and bright as if just now remembering she was not alone. She closed her mouth and nodded, casting her gaze back to the hearth.

We watched the fire together for a few minutes. My eyes lulled, the familiar sounds of the tavern below, along with the crackling of wood and full belly, calling for me to get some rest.

"I wonder who we'll meet tomorrow," she said casually.

"You mean, you wonder if we'll meet *him* tomorrow."

"Yes, I suppose I do."

Surprised by her miserable tone, I asked, "Don't you want someone to love you? Will you be happy when we find him, and he kisses your lips? You'll wake from your curse, free to love him back or not."

"No," she whispered.

"Why?"

"Because even if we do find this man, even if he does break this curse and saves us both from death, I am still to become a princess. I am still to live my life under my future husband's thumb."

"Ah," I puffed. "You wish to be free of your title just as much as your curse."

"Yes. I wish to return to my life in Moonstone Wood. I love my work crafting remedies for the Forestfae and experimenting with Moonstone crystals, so I wish my parents hadn't found me." She paused a moment, turning her head and resting her cheek on her transparent knee. "I'd rather you'd have found me than them. I'd take the curse over what my future as princess holds."

My brows rose. "You'd rather face death than become Princess of Riche?"

She shrugged. "They sound like the same fate to me."

Surprised and moved by her admission, my wings flared. "Tell me about your life in Moonstone Wood. What sorts of trouble have you gotten into since you left the sycamore tree?"

Her gaze shot to mine. "It wasn't I who left!"

I huffed a laugh. "I remember it perfectly, Phinie darling. You said, 'I must go, but I'll be back, Prince.'"

"I did come back! It was you who were gone!"

"I waited all day and night for you to come back to me. You never did. My mother found me as dawn approached. She forced me back to Brackish Castle, but I was able to leave you a—"

"A notched feather," she said softly. "I know. I found it the next day when I returned and waited for you to come back."

"I couldn't get away after that."

"I know. Well, I know now."

I hefted a heavy sigh. "And that was the end of it. Two children. Two *friends*," I amended, "playing and reading under an old sycamore tree before their lives moved on without the other."

"I wouldn't think you'd be so sentimental."

I leaned back on my hands casually. "I'm not. I just want to make sure we remember the events as they were." I quirked a brow her way. "Strangers don't share their first kiss either, Phinie. But childhood friends often do."

"You remember that, too?"

"I could never forget that."

The air felt too torrid, too sparked, too warm next to the fire. Seraphine Dupont was beautiful, and I remembered thinking the same thing at ten years old.

She was also a hidden princess, betrothed to a prince—though I wasn't sure that was still happening—and cursed by me, soon to be dead if we didn't find the one who could love her most. We had no time for these memories to bring forth whatever we'd never settled between us. I doubted she even remembered much of what it was like that summer—climbing the sycamore, telling each other jokes, reading books we had brought from our homes, and lying under the summer sun, my small wings wrapping around her once when she fell asleep.

No, I doubted she remembered those little details.

I convinced myself that I barely did.

CHAPTER 12

Seraphine

I SPENT THE NIGHT STRUGGLING TO TURN PAGES WITH my toes. I must have cursed this curse a hundred times, so thankful Korven was sleeping soundly instead of watching his *old childhood friend* attempt to pinch pages of his books with her newly solid, forever frozen feet.

Goddess be, he'd remembered more of our few days together than I would have guessed. It was nothing to ponder further, I reminded myself again, focusing on the events of the book I'd been reading for a few hours. According to the clock at his bedside, he'd slept longer than the previous night and dawn would soon arrive.

I rose from the floor, returning to the fire which glowed as mere embers. I didn't trust myself to lift more logs to keep it going and worried they'd all tumble to the floor, waking him and furthering my embarrassment.

What I really needed to do was focus. If my body was going to solidify bit by bit, it must be because we were getting closer to finding this person who could love me most. I wondered, sitting before the dying light, if my body back at the castle was slowly fading. I wondered if my feet had disappeared under the gargantuan dress I still wore. I wondered what rumors had spread now about the royal wedding being called off due to the princess's curse. I wondered if Korven's wings were still warm.

As if summoned by the thought, his eyes blinked. I just so happened to be staring stupidly at his face. His dark lashes fluttered open and he smiled. I caught it before I turned away, focusing back on the fire.

Without a word, he rose and stretched his arms and wings, before shuffling to the pile of wood, tossing more onto the embers and stoking the flames until the logs lit. I quietly watched his movements, attempting that focus again and failing miserably.

How did he remember so much of those few weeks when we were mere children? He was a young Ravenfae Prince and I'd been no more than a wild little human girl, living under the protection of the Forestfae. Maybe it was simply that you always remember your first kiss and we'd shared ours below that sycamore tree the last time we'd met.

"Did you read this?" he broke in the silence, holding up my favorite book of those scattered across the floor.

I nodded.

"And..." He glanced down at my feet propped up at the fire's hearth. "You turned the pages with your toes?"

I scrunched my nose, nodding again.

His chest held in his laugher, but he struggled to keep the blooming grin from his face.

"Resourceful, huh?" I said playfully.

He chuckled. "You surprise me more and more, Seraphine."

"How so?" I asked, rising to stand.

"I didn't know much about you when I flew here to deliver your curse. And who you are is not what I expected."

He pulled the spindle he had used to bestow the curse out of his pocket, and then pulled a wrapped bundle from his bag.

I sighed. "I hesitate to ask what you expect—what are you doing?" I cut myself off, curious when he pulled a tuft of wool from the wrapped brown paper. He sat on his bed, pulling at the mess of fibers until a long strand emerged.

He kept his eyes on his work, murmuring, "Spinning."

"Oh," I replied, still confused.

He hooked the strand onto his spindle, bending the sharp end I'd pricked my finger on so that it curled. He attached the long string of wool and began to spin, twisting the fibers so it wound around the shaft, creating a cop of yarn. I watched in nothing short of bemusement. The last thing I expected the very handsome, very grown up Ravenfae Prince of my childhood to do was spin wool into yarn.

"You were saying," he prodded, keeping an eye on his work.

"Yes, I...I don't remember what I was saying."

"You're surprised to see me use this spindle for actual spinning."

"Well...yes. I am surprised by that."

"So we both are surprising each other."

I could hear the smirk in his voice and I joined him, with a flirtatious, "I wonder what other surprises await."

His deep brown eyes slid slowly to my face, and he paused in his work. My cheeks suddenly burned. I'd flirted with plenty of men and fae before. This was different. The others had meant little more than flesh seeking pleasure. But this gaze I found myself more than wanting.

"Yes," he whispered, "I wonder."

I urged myself to speak, to change the subject and move on. I considered racing out of the room, suddenly afraid of what my heart did when he looked my way. Goddessdamn him, why did he look at me like that?

He cleared his throat, moving on for me. "We need to be back at the Burrow in an hour. We have another long day ahead of us."

"Alright," I said softly, returning to the fire to bask my toes in the heat.

We did have a long day ahead of us. And whatever it would bring, something comforting settled in my heart, knowing I'd still return to this room when the day was over.

CHAPTER 13

Korven

"WITHOUT A DOUBT, THE MOST INSURMOUNTABLE mountaintop was the tip of the Icenree. However, I did find myself atop its highest peak, and there I saw all of the Silver Isle. I could see our great realm of Revelry for miles and miles."

Lord Pilford of Wendlyn's voice echoed alone through the room. Beside me, Seraphine's blanket covered her chair, masking her feet at the bottom. With her arms folded at her chest, she scowled. I doubted mountain climbing was something she desired to pursue.

"Very interesting, Lord Pilford," I drawled. I finished the last spin for my current cop of yarn, setting the spun wool on the table next to the other five. One more tuft and I'd have enough. I pulled on the fibers, beginning again. "You seem to be quite adventurous. Tell me, what do you enjoy doing when you are actually at your estate?"

He stroked his red beard. "Well...that is...to be truthful, Prince Korven, I am never home."

"Ah. Thank you for your time, Lord Pilford. You may go."

"What exactly are you doing here with all of us?"

I lifted my gaze to really look at this bachelor. He was tall and well built with strong arms, like he really did climb frozen mountains regularly. But he was not the one for Seraphine. And he wasn't *that* good looking. I turned my head to meet her eyes, but she was watching Lord Pilford's face, the slightest corner of her mouth rising.

Frowning, I dropped my spindle and wool on the table, cracking my knuckles, getting her attention as I wanted. "Would you like more questions, then?"

"If you'd like to ask them, yes," Lord Pilford answered.

"I wasn't speaking to you."

"Apologies, but...then who were you speaking to?"

I didn't answer him, waiting for Seraphine's reply.

"Do we have a maybe list?" she asked.

I restrained my irritation. This man was never home. He climbed mountains and explored the wilderness. What in the realm's name would they even have in common? I rolled my shoulders, my wings flexing with the rest of me. "We could make one, if you like."

"Excuse me, Prince, but who are you speaking to? It is just you and I in this room."

Seraphine gave a slight nod and instead of crossing Lord Pilford of Wendlyn's name off the list, I drew a heart next to it with my quill.

She laughed, just as I'd hoped.

"Thank you for your time, Lord Pilford," I said, ignoring his previous question. "Please refrain from climbing any mountains or foraging the mountainsides for your own sustenance. I will be in touch."

"But you haven't explained what this is—"

I held up my hand to stop him. "Believe me, Lord Pilford, it is worth the secrecy."

Acknowledging the dismissal, he bowed and left, his face contorted with confusion.

"Really?" I started after the door was closed. "Is that what you'd prefer? A man to love you most atop a mountain in an entirely different kingdom than the one you'll rule?"

"He's the most interesting man we've met thus far. After all,"—she leaned closer to my chair, counting the names—"sixty-seven of them." Folding her arms and tapping that foot again, she added, "Maybe he'd change and stick around if he found that he loved me."

"People don't change, Seraphine," I lectured, resuming my spinning.

She laughed. "Says the Ravenfae Prince who can spin wool into yarn so expertly. Tell me, which woman did you change for who taught you that?"

"My sister."

I smirked in her silence.

"I...I didn't know you had one."

"I didn't when we were friends. She came along a little later."

"So, she's much younger?"

"Fifteen in a few months."

"And she taught you how to spin wool?"

"And knit," I added, chuckling at her surprise.

"You must care for her dearly to learn such a skill."

"I do," I said softly.

There was much to Morella that Seraphine would likely never know. My sister was a part of my life I'd keep and keep well to myself. Her future depended on it.

"I'm glad you have someone, then," she murmured. "I know it was a lonely childhood for you, too."

Her comment struck me somewhere inside. I frowned and continued spinning, my fingers pulling on the fibers of the twisted wool faster and faster as my lips pursed harder. I was...uncomfortable. Something I wasn't often. She had said something to make me tense and concerned...for her.

Swallowing back whatever lumped in my throat, I said, "We'll find him, Phinie. I promise you, we'll find someone to love you. You won't be alone anymore."

With that, she turned her body back towards the door, and I called the next name on the list.

CHAPTER 14

Seraphine

EIGHTY-NINE GENTLEMEN. THAT'S HOW MANY NAMES were crossed off the list in total. Three names had delicate little hearts next to their titles; three men seemed worth getting to know better. A good amount of me wanted to send them directly to my body waiting in the castle of Havenshire, have them kiss my cold lips, and be done with this. But it needed to be the right one. We needed to be sure because my betrothed had made it clear he would not allow a line of men to show up at his future queen's bedside, kissing her soundly. He could even be a problem when we figured we'd found the right one. Something told me Urik was considering letting me die if he himself could not have me.

Korven interviewed the fifth from last gentleman and my attention drifted. I focused on the ticking of his knitting needles, his fingers moving so deftly, quicker than I'd ever seen. Watching his skill, my thoughts drifted to his mysterious sister and what life had been like for Korven after we'd met. Would she grow up to bestow curses, too? What was her name? Did she look like Korven? Who was her father?

Most of the fae Goddesses of the Veil had children. All but

one. And each child usually had a different mortal father. I knew nothing of Korven's father and very little of his Ravenfae Goddess mother. Only what was told in one of my favorite books, but no one really knew how much of that story was true.

My education had been mostly my own doing. I'd spent my childhood at Fiola's court, learning all I could from her Forestfae, but most of them would rather roll down a grassy hillside than learn to read. When I had turned sixteen, I'd convinced her I was ready to find my own place. She knew of an abandoned cottage near the border of the Brackish Wood, unoccupied for about as long as I'd been living. A fae couple had lived there before their child was stolen from them. That was the story anyway. Regardless, it was my home, and I had been happy there. I didn't need many friends. I didn't need a constant companion, choosing instead to occasionally find a lover for a few nights when I was summoned to court.

I didn't need anybody.

Until now. On this day. In this moon cycle, when my life depended on just that.

Finding somebody.

"A good mystery sparks my fancy."

I tuned back into the conversation Korven was having with a portly man dressed impeccably, as they all were. His cheeks beamed a shiny red, and I didn't doubt it was from a nervous drink he'd had before his summons. He had all his hair, graying as it was, and a smile that was joyful—could be charming even.

"And tell me, Count Iru, what do you think of women who have the herbalist skill?"

"Herbalists?" The count pondered the question and I raised a brow at Korven. He'd never asked this one before.

The Count continued. "I suppose I haven't much thought

of them. But I use a salve for my sore calves at night, so I do appreciate that women of such skill exist."

Korven put whatever he was knitting in his lap, posing the quill over Count Iru's name, watching me for my decision. I twisted my lips to the side and took another look at the man. Perhaps we could read mysteries by the fire, and I could rub his calves every night in the salve I made regularly for sore muscles.

Goddess save me.

I couldn't see that as my future. As much as I tried to imagine these men in my life, loving me, I couldn't see any of them doing that. But what did I know? I'd never been loved. Regardless of how I had loved once, I didn't know the feeling of being loved in return, knowing a man was out there, waiting to come home to me. Wanting to come home to *me*.

I wouldn't cry. Not like this where Korven would see, think me too tired to continue, and wonder at his own fate being tied to such a woman.

"Can we...take a rest for a bit?" I asked.

His brow furrowed as he nodded while crossing Count Iru's name off the list. "Of course."

After he excused the Count, he rose, leaving through the red door at the tallest room of the manor. I was thankful to be alone. I was thankful to know he'd return.

I sighed heavily, the weight of it surprising even me. I rose onto my feet and the soft red blanket fell to the floor revealing...more of me.

My feet were there in my shoes as before, but now, I existed in the flesh up to my knees. Unfortunately, that meant my Goddessdamned dress existed as well. The material swished in an obnoxious sound as I walked to the window, peering out at the Count's carriage. He stepped in and left what was likely the most bizarre interview he'd ever had, none the wiser what it was actually for. The door to the room opened and I turned.

Korven leaned on the frame, a Ravenfae dressed in black against the sharp bite of smooth red paint. The colors didn't fit him. He appeared hard, but had shown me only soft in the few days I'd known him as an adult.

He took a deep breath. "Are we going to talk about it?"

I wasn't sure what 'it' he was referring to. The men we had met? The names he had marked to meet again? The fact that Count Iru had a large stain across his cravat from lunch? The kiss we'd shared at ten-years-old?

"Wh-what? Talk about what?"

He lifted himself from the door, walking towards me as if I was a gentle creature and easily spooked. "Just one thing. There's just one thing we need to discuss, right now, at this moment."

I wouldn't do it.

I. Would. Not. Cry. Crying alone when the loneliness of the life I loved became too heavy was one thing, but crying in front of him...that was something I would not allow myself to do.

I swallowed as he crept closer. My knees backed against the window seat, my obnoxiously loud gown crinkling in the movement. I gritted my teeth, unable to feel the strength of my jaw at all. "What do we need to discuss?" I asked, my voice a breathy tremble.

He lingered near, his legs crushing the layers of fabric even more. His eyes darted all around my face, stalling on my lips before lifting back to my eyes. A wild smirk lit his mouth as he said, "This ugly fucking dress."

CHAPTER 15

Korven

SERAPHINE'S LAUGHTER LIFTED THE WEIGHT BETWEEN us, lightening the air from my jest which really wasn't much of a jest at all, due to the blindingly truthful fact that her dress was indeed incorrigibly hideous.

"What do you have against all these bows, and lace, and layers?"

A playful grin lifted along her mouth and her tone was coy, flirtatious even. Good. She'd been feeling the heavy burden of our task and falling to it by the end of that last bachelor. I needed her spirits up. I needed her here with me so we could find this...this...

Asshole.

If she was returning more of herself to flesh and bone, we must be getting even closer, which angered me because all of these pricks didn't deserve a woman like Seraphine Dupont.

"I have many transgressions against such a dress," I started. "First, of all,"—I stepped back, the movement revealing the new ten inches of silk circling her legs—"this color. White does not suit you, Phinie darling."

She laughed, all signs of her quiet lamenting gone. "Are you calling me a soiled woman?"

"I would never," I teased. "But you cannot wear this color. You belong in soft hues. Pale pinks,"—I reached out as if to touch her golden hair, the color of wheat after harvest—"lavender, and creams."

"I didn't know you were paying close attention," she breathed.

There it was again. That strike against me, hitting me somewhere across the chest, forcing me to feel what I couldn't afford to feel.

"Surprised?" I murmured.

"Yes," she replied quickly. Her hazy violet eyes flicked across my form. "You should know, I didn't choose this dress. It was chosen for me, same as my betrothed, my future, and my curse. And now I'm forced to wear it. Perhaps for eternity if we can't find him and I d—"

"Don't." I cut her off. "Don't finish that word. You won't. We'll find him. We're getting close."

"It doesn't feel like we are."

I bent low, on my knees before her for the second time in two days. I rubbed the pads of my fingers on the layers of white fabric, reminding her, "This proves we are. Fiola said you'd return. This must be what she meant, the crafty old hag."

"Don't call her that."

"Why not?"

"She took care of me. All my life, she was the closest I had to a parent."

"She took care of you like my mother took care of me?"

Her shoulders slumped.

"May I?" I lifted some of the hem of her dress.

Nodding, she sat on the window seat, visibly gulping as I

patted my knee. The excitement that coursed through me as I lifted her gown was...annoying. And evident in the way my wings spread swiftly across my back, always the most dramatic part of me.

Except for maybe one other.

There was her leg, long and beautiful, creamy and soft, easily a part of a woman that could bring me to my knees. And that's just where I was.

Her intake of breath cut sharp and sexy—exactly what I wanted to hear as I touched the skin of her knee, cupping the back and smoothing my thumb over the curve. I couldn't look at her. If I looked at her, she'd read into my face, and I couldn't let her see the desire I felt I'd successfully hidden for days. "This is fascinating." I cleared my throat so it didn't sound so Goddessdamned rough. "I've never seen a curse and a Goddess's blessing fight like this. More of you will come. We'll be ready when it does."

I wrapped my hand around her ankle and placed her foot back on the floor. In haste, I rose, not daring to look back as I made my way across the room and settled into my seat. I picked up the list of names, pretending to read them over and adjusting myself hardening right there in that room where Seraphine Dupont returned in the flesh piece-by-perfect-fuck-ing-piece.

My eyes skimmed over the names of the absolute idiots we had met over the last two days. Each one was nothing compared to her. How could any of these men love her? Even the three she forced me to keep in mind were nothing more than simple men whose lives were meaningless. I couldn't see anything remotely special about any of them, and I sat there, irritated that she had.

She joined me a few minutes later and without catching

her eyes, I lifted the blanket back over her chair, hiding that a partial princess was in the room.

When I called in the next bachelor, the air stilled. I felt it. Goddessdamn him, I saw it too in the way Seraphine shifted slightly—almost imperceptibly—but my Ravenfae senses didn't lie.

"Duke Arthur of..." I glared at the parchment. I hadn't read it carefully enough this morning.

"Of Riche, Your Highness," the bastard finished for me.

For fuck's sake, he was from Seraphine's homeland. Tall, muscular, golden hair that curled slightly and bright blue eyes. A white scar lined his face from eyebrow to jaw. I turned my head, studying Seraphine's reaction intently, suddenly filled with an unbidden jealousy I barely understood. Her violet eyes looked him over thoroughly. But her lips did not form a smile. There was that, at least.

I cleared my throat, returning to my task—more than ever determined to get him out of this room as soon as possible. My first question wasn't a question at all, but an irritated command. "Tell me about yourself."

He smiled—*the prick*—and began to speak freely in a rich tenor that swept through the room. "You know my title and where I'm from, Prince Korven, but I admit,"—he laughed, sliding his hands into his pockets—"I do not know exactly what I'm doing here. I only just arrived in Havenshire last week to attend the marriage of Prince Urik and Princess Seraphine."

The princess in question froze.

"And did you attend the marriage?" I asked.

"Unfortunately, no. My mother took ill the night before, and I needed to tend to her care. We brought very few of our staff with us and she needed me, so..." He took an unprompted step forward. "My apologies if I'm misunderstanding, but may I inquire as to what these interviews are regarding? No one in this club seems to know."

Ignoring his question, I continued, "What was the last book you read?"

Amusement crossed his features and Seraphine sat straighter to listen.

"I brought several with me." He pulled a small cloth bound book from his inner pocket and set it on the table—again, unprompted. "I most often read books of adventure. Occasionally the sciences. Faekind history is always intriguing." He tapped the cover of the worn book, obviously beloved. "But this one I keep here. With me at all times."

"What is it?" Seraphine whispered without the slightest movement.

I didn't ask her question. I just stared at the man. Seraphine smacked my foot under the table with hers.

"What is this book you so conveniently keep in your jacket pocket?" I was on to him. A duke of her kingdom just happened to waltz in carrying a book around? I admitted he was handsome. Too handsome. Men like that grew up with an air of arrogance and a long list of women who had occupied their beds. I didn't trust him. I didn't fucking like him.

"It's an old story. My favorite. You may know it—Cursed Goddess of the Veil."

Fuck. This. Duke.

Seraphine gasped beside me. It was too perfect. Far too perfect for me to believe any of it. Because though we'd been forced together only days ago, I wanted to protect her. Was it guilt from the curse I had delivered? Was it simply curiosity as to how this would end? I knew that wasn't it. I felt both of those things, but stronger than anything was this need to protect the girl I had met so many years ago in the cool air of spring, in a short moment of my life span I wouldn't forget for the next fifteen years.

The duke observed my face and a smile crept across his mouth, the corners of his blue eyes crinkling. "You know it, then," he added.

"Of course, I know it," I snapped. "We both know which Goddess it's about."

My mother. My mother's story. Parts of the tale were true. She'd never told me which parts, though. But there was something more disturbing about the book in front of us than that it depicted some of the downfall of the Ravenfae Goddess Reshina; the book was Seraphine's favorite. She had read it to me that spring under that sycamore tree, and the fact that he kept it in his fucking pocket—

"Ask him a detail about the story," she demanded.

Good. She was on to him, too.

"In this book, what does the Goddess of the Veil request as payment for her fate?" His face paled and his eyes narrowed. In his pause, I didn't give him much time to respond. "Well? You keep it in your pocket, so I assume you've read it multiple times." A merciless grin lifted my lips. I had him.

"A rose," he said quickly.

Fuck.

I turned to Phinie, desperate to see that she wasn't falling for this swindler.

She cleared her throat. "Keep his name. Let's move on."

Nodding, I hesitantly circled his name. I wasn't drawing a Goddessdamn heart next to it.

"Are we alone?" the duke all but whispered.

"What?" I jabbed, tossing the quill on the table.

"She's here, isn't she?"

Before I could stop him, he pulled the blanket trailing on the floor under the desk, revealing over twelve inches of

Seraphine. I heard the squeak of her chair as she rose, but missed anything she did next.

I shifted into a raven over the table, turning back to Ravenfae in a matter of seconds, pinning the duke against the door. Hand around his throat, my fist met his gut and his breath left his lungs. "You are young, Duke of Riche," I purred above his marred face. "I would think you'd like to experience more of your pathetic life."

"I'm sorry," he said, without even a hint of concern.

"I don't doubt it," I squeezed his throat and his face began to turn a mottled crimson, matching the door behind him. He didn't budge. He didn't grovel. Instead, his eyes darted to where Seraphine stood.

"I'm sorry, Princess," he choked. "I acted rashly. It won't happen again."

"I know it won't," I said for her. "If you do anything so stupid again, that mistake will be your last."

"Korven."

I turned at her call. Her arms were folded at her chest with a scowl across her face as I practically murdered the one man we'd met who had said all the right things so far. I shoved him back against the door and returned to my chair, shifting from faekind to raven and back again just to remind him of my power.

The duke adjusted his jacket, stepping up to the table and taking his book. "I apologize again, Princess Seraphine. It was not my intent to hurt you in any capacity." He tucked the book into his pocket and swept back the strands of hair that had fallen loose. "I will go."

I took up my knitting, furious, needing to occupy my hands before they found themselves in places they shouldn't.

"Make him stay. I have more questions," she commanded.

"What?" I growled.

"I want to know how he guessed."

"No."

"Korven."

"Can you hear her?" Arthur asked, his eyes darting to where Seraphine was sitting.

I gritted my teeth. "I can see her too, you fucking piece of shi—"

"*Korven*." Maybe she didn't want to be called princess, but she could command like one.

"Please," he begged, "forgive me. I didn't know."

I continued looping spun yarn across the clack of my needles. My nail beds pressed white in my fury. Seraphine laid her ghostly hand on my arm, tapping the edge of my boot once with her foot.

I breathed in and out through my nose, setting my needles down. She kept her hand on my arm as I folded mine on the table. "If you tell a single soul what you discovered here today, you will not live for long after."

He nodded. "I won't say a word."

"If I hear one rumor, one whisper of this, I know who to find and whose throat to slit."

"Seraphine," he said, ignoring my threat. "You've been cursed. I've heard...around that you collapsed on the night of your wedding and you reside in Castle Havenshire. But you're here, now, looking for someone. Will you tell me why?"

"You don't get to ask the questions," I bit.

"Tell him," she replied.

"You trust too easily, Phinie."

"You don't trust enough to end this. Tell him...*please*."

Fuck if my chest didn't ache from her ask. "Seraphine would like me to tell you what we are looking for, Duke of *Riche*."

He smiled at the space where she sat.

I ground my teeth before explaining. "The Princess Seraphine of Riche must be kissed to break her curse and live."

He frowned, bemused. "Why hasn't Prince Urik done so?"

"It's not just any kiss she needs, obviously. It must come from the one who loves her most."

His face fell and he addressed her again. "You have no one in your life to kiss you as such?"

Phinie shook her head and I mimicked the movement. I placed my hand over where hers rested on my arm. It was cold there in the space her spirit occupied, but she smiled at me in return.

Arthur cleared his throat and continued his questions. "And you're trying to find this...gentleman? The one who can love you most? This seems like an impossible task."

I huffed a laugh. "In current company, yes."

Ignoring my jab, she said, "Ask if he'll meet us again. Tomorrow."

"I don't think we should," I said in return, glaring his way.

"There's something to him, Korven. He feels connected to this and he's the best we have."

I lifted my hand, gesturing. "*This*? This is the best we've got?"

Her nostrils flared and she took her hand away. "I'm the one who gets full say in this. Tell him to meet us tomorrow. Now."

"Fine." I took up my needles, taking a moment to count stitches before looking up at the duke who had sparked her interest far more than mine.

"Princess Seraphine would like to see more of you tomorrow. I would like you to leave."

I felt the kick at my boot again and ignored it.

The duke blew a breath of air out of his lips, smiling at where Seraphine sat. She looked up at him with her own grin.

"Alright. I'm willing to try this. Truly, I am sorry, Princess. Sorry for my actions just now and sorry for your curse. If I can break it..." he trailed. "I will do what I can to help you. I will meet you again tomorrow. Do you have a place in mind?"

I opened my mouth to speak when both of them said, "The library."

Fucking bastard.

Seraphine laughed and Arthur waited for my reply.

"Fine. Noon. Go."

He turned to the door, calling back before he left. "It was a pleasure to meet you, Princess Seraphine."

CHAPTER 16

Seraphine

THE MOMENT THE CRIMSON DOOR CLOSED, I TURNED on him. "You made that far worse than it needed to be."

He counted more stitches. "He's a prick."

"He's a Duke of Riche who caught onto what was going on here, unlike every other man we've met." I started listing on my fingers. "He reads, he carries a book around in his pocket, he's from my kingdom, he cares about his mother."

"You don't know that."

"He said he missed the wedding to care for her."

"He said as much."

"You don't believe him. Why?"

Korven tossed his needles and knitted yarn to the table. "Word has spread of your curse. Not the details, but the state your body is in at Castle Havenshire. And here shows up a Ravenfae Prince, bestower of curses, interviewing the gentry of the Havenshire Kingdom, asking questions lacking just enough detail as to leave out what these interviews are really about. He has half a brain, I'll give him that. But it's too convenient. He shows up with your favorite book in his jacket pocket? No, Phinie, I don't believe him."

"You remember that it's my favorite book?" I asked.

"It was when you were ten."

It was then. It was now.

"I'm not saying he's the one to break the curse," I continued. "But I am saying I liked him."

Korven gave me a withering look.

"You have to admit he's handsome," I said, holding back a snicker.

"I don't have to admit that."

My jaw dropped. "You're jealous!"

"Of a man like that? Never."

His fingers worked quickly, forming more of the tube he knitted. I wasn't sure exactly what he was making or why he felt the need to do it right now, but his words didn't fool me. Knitting...whatever it was acted more as a distraction than anything. He didn't like the duke. But he didn't like him well before Arthur had swept the blanket from the chair.

Why would Korven be jealous? This is what he wanted. This is what he needed to get himself out of this curse with me. Arthur had acted rashly exposing my secret, but he had also been apologetic, thoughtful, and clever. His obvious joy of reading matched my own and he was handsome. In a dangerous sort of way. That scar down his face...I wanted to ask about it.

I examined that thought. It was pure curiosity, nothing more. For though he'd said the right things, proved he and I could likely get along, I'd felt nothing more, really.

Korven stared at me as I processed my thoughts.

"You're thinking about him," he mumbled.

"Yes," I replied with a sly smile.

"Fine," he grumbled, "we'll see what other pieces of your past he'll pull out of his jacket tomorrow. Crystals? Salve recipes?"

I laughed, goading him further. "Would be nice. I've been looking for one for warts."

FIVE MORE MEN LATER AND WE'D EXCUSED THEM ALL, each one with us for no more than five minutes before we decided they wouldn't work.

I stretched my legs under the table, letting the blanket slide off my dress in a heap on the floor. "Who knew finding a man to love me would be so exhausting," I yawned, covering my mouth at the last second before Korven saw me.

"You're getting tired. Maybe now that there's more of you reappearing, you'll be able to sleep." We both glanced down to my legs, but no more of me had appeared.

"Ha," he uttered, folding the blanket and placing it back on the window bench.

"What?"

"No more of you has returned today."

"So?"

"If the ever-so-charming duke was the right man to love you, wouldn't there be more of you by now?"

"I never called him charming," I replied, rising and ready to tease him some more.

"But you would?" he asked, taking my bait.

I shrugged, waiting for him to open the door. "Perhaps. We'll find out tomorrow. At noon. At the library."

Something about seeing him obviously disgusted by the idea lit a fire in my cold bones. Not one other gentleman had sparked this in him. None had said all the right things like Arthur.

Again, I wondered why Korven seemed so irked. Breaking the curse would benefit him, too. So, why the irritation? Why did I see jealousy in his eyes as he held the handle of the crimson door, staring me down.

Softly, he said, "Are you looking forward to tomorrow, Phinie darling?"

"Yes," I replied in a squeak. Goddessdamn him. His dark lashes drifted lower as he slid his gaze down my body, all the way to my legs covered by yards of silk.

"To see him again?"

"No," I answered quickly, letting my grin widen on my face when I saw that same surprise in his eyes. "I've just never visited a library."

I SHOOK MY HEAD AND CROSSED MY ARMS, READY TO stomp. "I'm not taking it."

"Yes, you are."

"No. I don't need it like you do. I'm fine right here." I pointed to the floor where I'd managed to pull a blanket from the surprisingly well-stocked, half-broken bed in Korven's room.

"Get in the bed, Phinie." He had taken one look at my little nest on the floor after eating a quick dinner downstairs and demolished my plans instantly.

"Korven," I returned, just as stubborn. "I don't even have half of my body. I will not sleep long and I will be perfectly warm if I stay next to the fire." I pointed to the narrow bed, stocked with one lumpy pillow and three more blankets, albeit a bit threadbare. I stood my ground. "*You* are sleeping in this bed tonight, end of discussion."

"You can't force me to do that."

"Just as you can't force *me*," I snapped back. It was a silly argument, really. He was a full-grown Ravenfae Prince, and I was about one-third of a human woman. My legs ached, heavy and tired, but I wasn't about to take his bed from him.

He unfastened his black shirt, pulling the hem from his waistband and lifting the back off his wings. His movement was swift, determined, as if he'd known we'd eventually come to this impasse. He dropped his shirt on the floor and strode to me, bending to gather the mounds of fabric in his arms and lifting me up so my knees bent in the crook of his elbow.

"You wouldn't dare," I gasped, attempting to kick but with no real force of muscle from my thighs.

He all but tossed me onto the bed where I immediately began to scoot to the edge to stagger back to my cozy blanket on the floor.

Without a word, he leapt onto the bed, pressing his long legs down so they crossed mine. A staggered cry of injustice escaped me as I fruitlessly attempted to move my legs out from underneath his.

"I'm a heavy sleeper," he said. "I won't be leaving this bed anytime soon." He pressured my legs to stay still as we made an awkward X with our limbs. He fluffed the pillow, then pulled a blanket at the bottom of the bed up over the both of us.

I sat there in awe and anger, the blanket and his legs warming me with the purity that was the heat of another body.

"Goodnight," he chuckled, ignoring my narrowed eyes on his face. Without another word, he blew out the candle on his bedside table, leaving the small fire as the only light in the room.

I...liked the pressure, I admitted, just moments after I noticed his chest breathing deep. I didn't want to enjoy the weight of him. I didn't want to adore that he had forced me to sleep in his bed as more of my flesh and bones returned.

But there I was, smiling to myself. Only allowing a little grin, knowing he couldn't see it. I had come to terms with this particular Ravenfae being the one whose fate was tied to mine, but his actions of protecting me—his jealous nature revealing itself for the first time—these were matters I needed to mull over.

My eyes grew heavy. The exhaustion from days without sleep settled in on my soul. The bed was small. He took up most of it, especially with his feathered wings sprawled out behind him.

I reached out as if I could touch him, again allowing myself this one thing while he slept deeply. Each feather looked soft and dark, a secret world I wanted to explore in the veins and downy barbs.

He'd given me one of his feathers once. Left it at our tree. I had kept that feather for years and years until the day a swift wind had taken it from the pages of my open book. I had felt sorrow at the time, watching it fly into the forest trees of Moonstone Wood. That was five years ago. I had changed much since then.

My eyes drooped lower. I settled myself at an awkward angle along the wall where the bed met the wood planks of the Rose and Briar. I lifted my gaze to see his serene face one more time, allowing myself just one more permission; if I dreamed, I hoped I dreamed of him.

I WOKE TO THE CLACKING OF KNITTING NEEDLES. I refused to open my eyes. I refused to move from where my legs were tangled with his, no longer just underneath, but entwined. I held onto my dream. A dream of warm feathers and flying through a starlit sky. I blushed thinking of what else had happened in that dream with this Ravenfae Prince I was currently resting with. The most salacious of thoughts and scenarios ran through me, and I let them.

More of me had appeared in the night. I knew because I could feel the heavy weight of his thigh pressed over mine. I felt the warmth of him nestled between my legs, and Goddessdamn him, I didn't want to move from the bed he had forced me into.

So, I listened instead. I pretended to sleep when what I really needed to do was quell the ache inside. I knew some parts of me had not returned or I'd feel actual discomfort between my legs for what my heart begged to do with the Ravenfae Prince who had cursed me.

I couldn't have him. I'd never have him. Even if there was more of me to seek the touch of his skin, I knew he was not mine. I knew he never would be and that sobered me from my dream. We had a curse to break and a duke to meet. Dreams were for the Goddessblessed, not the Goddesscursed.

I stretched my arms and legs, pretending I had just woken. The blanket that was draped over the two of us poofed ridiculously with the amount of wedding dress that had also appeared in the night.

He allowed my stretch, adjusting his legs as I moved mine,

but not enough to let them go. I sat up and covered my yawn. "Good morning," I said sweetly.

"Good afternoon." He lifted his eyes once over his reading glasses to give me a smirk before continuing to the clack of his needles.

"Afternoon?" I questioned.

"It's past one."

"Shit! We're late!" I cried, scrambling in the blankets to free my legs from his.

He grabbed my gown, hauling me back onto the bed. "I've taken care of it. We're meeting the duke at two instead. Lay back down before you trip yourself."

I landed back with a puff, my legs bent through his. I gave him a huff and kicked the blanket from us both to study my strange ascent back to normalcy.

Lifting my voluminous skirts, we stared at my feet, my shins, knees, and thighs all returned to their usual peachy hue. I was flesh again all the way up to where my thighs met, my undergarments still transparent like the rest of me. I didn't care if he saw. I didn't care that I still wore what Prince Urik had gifted me on our wedding day in a white box wrapped in a white ribbon.

Now, I was glad I had put on the undergarment that wasn't much coverage instead of tossing it into the fire like I was initially tempted to do. I glanced at Korven, but he wasn't sneaking a look at the strings of fabric at the center of my legs; he was watching my face. His dark brown eyes, almost black, bore into mine with an intensity and hunger I recognized in a man's face.

If I had been fully flesh, a chill would have slid through me despite the warmth of the room and his legs under mine. I shifted, bending my legs at the knee and sliding them across his own. His gaze dropped to where almost half of my body draped across him.

"There's more of you," he said, tossing his glasses to the small table and setting his needles in his lap.

Wrapping his hand around one of my ankles, he lifted it, pulling me toward him and I cried out, sliding across the bed until my legs were folded in his lap. Keeping his grip on my ankle, he asked, "Why is there more of you, Seraphine?"

I gulped. There wasn't enough of me for this. There wasn't nearly enough skin to slide against his own. I didn't have the hands to grip him, or the mouth to slide along his neck—

"Seraphine."

He interrupted my thoughts. My mouth parted, my face no doubt showing every imaginable desire across it.

"We're...we're getting closer to finding him," I whispered. Goddessdamn him, I could barely speak as his hand roamed from my ankle up the back of my calf, gripping the back of my knee.

"Did you dream of the duke, Seraphine?"

His question dripped with jealousy and a possessiveness I didn't quite understand. Prince Korven wanted me. Prince Korven thought he couldn't have me, but that was so far from the truth.

"No," I started, shifting my leg so his hand found my thigh. "I didn't dream of the duke."

He licked his bottom lip. "Prince Urik, perhaps?"

Now he was playing with me. It must have been obvious— my want of him written plainly across my ghostly face.

In a flash of frustration and anger, I yanked my legs from his grip, tangling them further in the mounds of fabric. I rolled from his lap, managing to avoid his next attempt to grab me and keep me on his ramshackle bed in his cramped room that I had to share because I was half a person and he had done that to me.

There I was, lusting after the Goddessdamn harbinger of my spirit being pulled from my body to wander this Goddessdamned kingdom to somehow come across a man who could love me most.

The fury of it all rose to an unmistakable rage, and I no longer cared to tangle what parts I could with the Ravenfae Prince, or with any duke, or potential gentleman. I hated how helpless I was, relying on him, relying on Fiola's response to the curse, and acting as if this new form was some sort of blessing instead of just one curse upon another.

I wanted to go home. I wanted to open the door to my cottage and find peace at the familiar sight of drying flowers upturned above the mantle. I wanted to put the kettle on the fire hook and brew some of my favorite chamomile tea with lemon and lavender, reading a new book I'd bought at the Moonstone market.

Fuck this prince, fuck this duke, and fuck this dress.

I flung myself from the bed, my legs catching in the endless white fabric, tripping me just as he predicted would happen. I caught myself on the floor with my knees before falling completely with a loud, "Oomph."

Strong arms lifted me almost instantly, sitting me back onto the edge of the bed. I opened my mouth to protest, ready to claim to not need his help, regardless of how much I actually did, but he shook his head, silencing me. Layer by layer, he rolled the fabric of my gown up to my lap until my legs were exposed and he could inspect the scrape across my knee. He traced around the torn skin, wiping the bead of blood that began to drip.

"I believe I warned you this would happen just minutes ago."

"It's this Goddessdamned gown!" I gritted in exasperation. "I hate it! I hate the chains it represents. I hate the symbol that binds me to a life I would never choose for myself."

In a flash, he pulled a dagger from his pocket, flicking it between his fingers and holding it poised above the bustle of bows rolled up to my thighs. "Give me the word and it's gone."

Without hesitation, I nodded, adding, "Do it. Get it off me, Korven."

He went to work, slicing his blade through the yards of expensive silk, hacking and cutting away what had materialized with parts of me returned, so careful around my skin. As soon as the front of the dress fell away, I stood, providing access to the rest of me so he could rip and tear at the shackles I'd worn since the day of my wedding.

I turned as the last swaths of fabric hit the floor, my breath heavy, my anger subsiding. My legs bare and chilled before him.

My wedding gown was ruined. Destroyed by the man who had ensured I would not be marrying into the Kingdom of Havenshire. Tatters of bows, pearls, and lace littered the floor. I stood there, catching my breath—not from the destruction of my cage—but from the Ravenfae kneeling before me, his breath just as heavy, his eyes locked on mine.

I knew what I would have done.

If we'd been shoved together in some other way, some other instance that didn't involve a curse and a body so slowly reforming, I would have kissed him.

I would have slid into his lap on the floor, tangling our limbs together. I would have run my hands over the underside of his wings just to feel the veins, just as soft as the feather he had gifted to me all those years ago. I would have touched him for hours and taken anything he'd give me.

"Are you cold, Phinie darling?" he whispered.

I gasped as he lifted a hand to the top of my thigh, right underneath the new hem of my dress, inches from the one part of me I wanted back so badly.

He slid his fingers across my legs, running his hand down and around the back of my scraped knee, caressing around the wound with his thumb and blowing softly over the torn skin.

"Yes," I breathed in reply.

"Sit."

Immediately, I fell to the bed. He reached around me, grabbing his knitting. Pulling the needles from the woven yarn, he cut the string, tying it with deft fingers.

"These are for you." He lifted his work, finally giving me a good look at what he'd been working on for two days.

Stockings.

Soft, cream stockings.

In shock, I let him lift my foot to rest on his knee. He bundled the stocking in his hand, and I pointed my toes so he could slip it onto my foot.

And up his hands went.

Over my calf, carefully around my split knee, trailing up the skin of my thighs with the softest wool.

I felt the room disappear. No sounds came from below, no heat from the crackling fire. No curses, no titles, no impending doom to complete a task I cared little for.

The room faded with everything around it, leaving just a hidden princess and the Ravenfae Prince she had fallen for a very long time ago, keeping her safe, keeping her warm, unknowingly keeping her his as she always would be.

CHAPTER 17

Korven

I took my time, holding her legs over my shoulders as she laughed in the most beautiful way, her arms outstretched as if she had wings herself. Her knees bent pressed to my neck, and I let myself occasionally rub a thumb over her ankles as I held her in place.

There was more of Seraphine Dupont.

More of her had materialized as she lay tangled in my bed.

More of her soft skin had shown itself wrapped through my legs, and Goddess be, it had been painful to leave her side and send word we'd be late. But she had been sleeping so hard, I knew if I got back quickly, I'd still have a chance to lay in a warm bed with the woman I could never have.

We soared through the afternoon sun, the promise of summer still a few weeks away from the kingdom of Havenshire. The Krukus Mountains shone in the distance with white peaks and tree-lined slopes. Just beyond the jagged cliffs were both of our homes where we'd met so long ago.

I hadn't had a sister back then, and now, I couldn't forget what I was doing and who all this was for. Seraphine's curse was just a sidestep before I got back on track. There was more than one reason I couldn't have her, and I needed to remember that.

Her gasp as we soared near the tall spires was a breath of delight. "That's the library?" she called as I circled us over the towering pinnacles.

"The largest in the human kingdoms. Built over two centuries ago, according to a scribe I met last week."

She rocked on my shoulders, urging me to land. "It's magnificent! And books are loaned to anyone?"

"Well…" I began, touching down behind the building and pulling my black cloak over my shoulders, leaving half of her transparent form riding above my head. "No, actually. Patrons of Havenshire are required to access the thousands of books *inside* the library."

"But you said the books in your room are from…oh," she finished.

I pulled three out of my satchel, waving them in front of her face. "What they don't know are missing, won't hurt them."

"You thief!" she squealed, jabbing my ribs with her heel.

I caught her ankle wrapped in the stocking I'd made for her. "Thief I may be, but a poor one at that. I'm returning them, aren't I?"

"What if you're caught?" she whispered harshly, as if one of the library patrons could hear her as I opened the door.

I answered with a shrug. "What if I'm caught?"

I took us through the entranceway and let her take it in for a moment. Out of all of the Havenshire I'd seen, this building was the most impressive. The whole of the inside was encased in beautiful delicate scrollwork of dark wood carved in sworls and intricate patterns across the parquet flooring. The library entrance lay at street level, whereas most of the stacks and shelves rose four stories above us, each section with its own massive hallway, complete with desks to study.

If you provided proof of status to the clerk, you could pay a mark to borrow an oil lamp for your stay in the more dimly lit hallways.

Thankfully, I possessed enough magic to never need a lantern.

"I don't know where we should even start," she murmured.

"We have a good thirty minutes before the duke arrives."

She bucked at my shoulders again. "Then hurry! I want to see everything!"

I laughed to myself, sliding my hand up and down her leg before I realized I was doing it for my own sake, not hers.

"Any requests on where to begin?" I asked, twisting my head up to see her face. Her lips were parted as she surveyed the halls of books. She lifted her hand to her forehead as if to shield herself from sunlight, turning her head back and forth.

I chuckled, wishing I'd told the prick of a duke to fuck off for the rest of the day. I wanted this day for us. I wanted to spend hours here with Seraphine, pulling books from the shelves when she wanted to read them. We could walk down each and every hallway so she could read the spines, direct me where to go, and squeal happily again and again.

My Seraphine loved books.

But she wasn't my Seraphine. At least not for much longer.

"There!" She interrupted my thoughts, pointing across the hall to the left at the section labeled Revelry History.

"Aye-aye, Captain," I replied, earning a questionable glance from the desk clerk and another laugh from the woman I held onto for as long as I could.

Four halls in, we had to stop after I'd caught a glimpse of the Duke of Riche standing at the entrance and checking his pocket watch more than once.

Disappointed, Seraphine agreed it was time to meet with him. I lifted her from my shoulders, placing her body on a cushioned chair at the end of the secluded aisle. I unfastened my cloak and covered her legs, draping the rest of the wool over the back of the chair.

I bent, pondering what we both knew had happened in the thirty minutes since we'd arrived at the library. I got to work with the cloak, covering all of her legs to keep them away from the duke's wandering eyes.

Tucking the ends underneath her thighs, I kept my eyes to my task, finally speaking up as she watched me in silence. "There's more, Seraphine," I spoke softly in the dim light of the flame I kept suspended over the desk. "Why is there more of you?"

I let my gaze drift to her face, sliding my hands along the form of her under my cloak, my fingers roaming over newly formed hips.

She swallowed and looked down at herself, crossing one leg over the other, despite my attempt to keep her tucked in and hidden. Shrugging too casually, she cleared her throat. "I suppose the arrival of Arthur has...encouraged more of my body to return."

"The fuck it did," I growled back.

"Prince Korven!" the duke called behind me. The bastard had come looking for us.

I held her gaze a moment more before rising and turning, crossing my arms and nodding toward the duke practically sprinting our way.

"And Princess Seraphine..." He grinned. "Is she...oh."

He caught sight of her long legs, crossed and draped in the stockings I'd made to keep her warm. The delicate shape of her foot rocked gently.

I opened my mouth to order the duke to get lost when he stepped around me and pulled another chair away from the desk. "May I?" he asked, gesturing with an open hand to the seat in question.

"Yes," Seraphine replied.

He continued to wait.

"Korven," she growled.

"She said yes," I responded, leaning against a shelf, watching his every move.

He thanked her and sat, leaning forward on his legs and stealing a glance at the drape of her calf across her knee.

"This will be...difficult, won't it?" he said. "It's unfortunate we require a chaperone to get to know one another."

I scoffed, my wings rustling in irritation. "Even if you could hear and see her, I wouldn't let you within five feet without a chaperone."

The bastard grinned back at me. "Thank you for protecting her so devoutly, Prince Korven."

Before I could even begin my next stream of curses, Seraphine uncrossed her legs, tucking them up underneath her, and quickly saying, "Ask him if he has any other family besides his mother."

I gritted my teeth, scowling in his direction. "She wants to know about your family."

He folded his hands, replying to where her face should be.

"I have no family. None except my mother. And she is not long for this world."

"I'm sorry," Seraphine replied. "What about friends? Social activities?"

A saccharin grin lit my face. "Do people enjoy your company, Duke, or do you lack friendships as well as a living family tree?"

Two heads turned and glared my way.

"Your Ravenfae chaperone doesn't seem to like me much, Princess."

She pursed her lips, but replied, "No, he certainly doesn't." Then, she retorted to me, "If you do not say exactly what I say, this will never work and we'll both be dead soon, so I demand that you follow through with this plan we agreed upon."

I loved her ire. I considered keeping it going, shooting back something about how much I didn't trust this duke without a family—and more than likely—without friends.

"Fine," I caved. "She would like to know if you have any friends and what, if any, social activities you find yourself in."

"Ah," he chuckled, "I do have a few close friends, but I'm afraid I'm not the type to attend many parties or dances. Perhaps it's why I've been a bachelor for so long."

Before Phinie could ask, I did it for her. "How old are you?"

"Thirty-seven this fall."

"Where did you get the scar?" I asked next, ignoring her hiss of my name.

"Fell from a tree about ten years ago."

"Ten years ago, you were still older than Princess Seraphine is now." I continued my inquiry. "What happened to your father? Siblings? Aunts? Cousins? Surely it is not just you as duke of an estate in Riche."

"Unfortunately, Prince Korven, it is just me. There is a

townhouse in Riche I occupy most of the year. However, in the past few months, I have been visiting my ailing mother at our castle in Heartstone Wood. It's a drafty old place."

"You didn't say what happened to your father."

"I had imagined you'd realized he's dead."

"How?"

"Rasping Sickness."

"How long ago?"

"Ten years."

"Is that why you fell out of the tree?"

"No."

"In Cursed Goddess of the Veil, how long ago was my mother's fate cast?" I'd stump him here. Even if he had studied the book, it was unlikely he'd done the math, expecting this question.

Without missing a beat, he replied with an accurate, "Five-hundred and twelve years."

Phinie had gone quiet, her eyes darting back and forth between us.

I stepped closer, standing over him, as imposing a figure of a Ravenfae Prince as I could manage. "You show up to the Burrow, a place you don't regularly occupy, with a title, land, and her favorite fucking book in your jacket pocket with no family to claim, no wild past, no ring on your finger, and you just happen to enjoy the quiet and reading?" I bent closer. "Do you see, Duke of Riche, why I do not trust you? Why I question you and your intentions with the princess of your kingdom? Nothing fits into place that perfectly."

He turned to Seraphine with a broad smile. "Your favorite book is Cursed Goddess of the Veil?"

She didn't respond. She didn't so much as look at him. She stared at me with bright eyes, something glistening in them I hadn't yet seen. Her breasts rose and fell heavily above the enormous satin bow at her chest.

I swallowed, forcing myself to look away. "What is your purpose in coming here, Duke? What do you get out of this?"

Finally, he faltered, taking a breath to answer before slumping back in his seat. "You've got me there, Prince Korven. I came because of...curiosity. Because of this strange situation the Princess of Riche has found herself in. I live a lonely life. One I have chosen to live, but if I could find..." he trailed off and I silently dared him to say the words. He chose not to. "If I could help lift this curse, I would do it. There's no need for hostility. No need for demanding such a thorough look at my life, though I appreciate why you're so ardently searching for holes in my answers. I am here to get to know Princess Seraphine Dupont. That is all. No commitment, no confessions of feelings. She is most intriguing, so far as I know."

"You don't know," I shot back.

"*Korven.*"

Her command of my name drew me. Instantly, I straightened, turning to her chair.

She continued, "I think that's enough today. Please tell him verbatim, 'Thank you for joining us today, Arthur. I feel the same. No commitment, no confessions of feelings needed. If you would like, please come back tomorrow, same time. Prince Korven will be a more willing chaperone then, I assure you.'"

I sighed heavily and repeated her words exactly.

Another of those charming smiles graced his face. The white scar running down his cheek giving him more of a roguish look.

He stood and bowed before Seraphine. "I'm looking

forward to it, Princess. I do hope I've conducted myself appropriately in such royal company."

Seraphine inclined her head, but I gave no indication of such a thing. He turned on his heel and left, cracking his neck as he swept past the corner down the long hall and out of sight.

I made sure he left the library. Of course, I did.

"Korven."

She called to me again, her voice like a pull back to her side where I slumped into the opposite chair, running my hands down my face. I needed to get a grip and react with less hostility, less outright disdain the next afternoon. This curse was in need of breaking, and we were running on little time.

I blew air out of my mouth, nibbling on my bottom lip. "I'll do better."

"You'll do better," she repeated.

"I hate him."

She laughed, slipping her legs back out from underneath her body. "You hate him."

I shook my head, leaning forward on my knees. "That won't change. He could be a fucking saint of the Veiled Ones and I'd still hate him."

"He's no saint."

"How can you tell?" I said in a snide response.

She hummed, crossing her long leg back over her knee. "There's something he's not saying. I can hear it in the way he doesn't talk about...whatever it is. It's a very mysterious thing."

"You're intrigued by mysterious dukes, then?" I was leaning so close now, my body but a few inches away from the stocking I'd pulled onto her legs a mere hour ago.

She shook her head with a sly smile. "No. I prefer a jealous prince."

"Careful now," I growled. "Your words are sounding more and more like an invitation."

Her lips parted and she uncrossed her legs, lifting a foot to slide across the seat on the side of my chair. My cloak fell away from her easily, even after all that careful tucking her away from wandering eyes.

My eyes wandered, though. She wanted them to. That much was clear as she lifted her other leg, placing the bottom of her foot on the other side of me, sliding it down the seat as well. She kept her knees closed to me, teasing with the most seductive smirk across her lips.

"And what would you say to an invitation?"

I caught her foot at my side, bringing it to my lap where I rubbed the arch with the pads of my thumbs. "What kind of invitation are we talking about, Seraphine?"

It was a dangerous game. One neither of us could afford to play, yet neither of us seemed able to decline.

Pulling out of my grasp, she slid her stocking feet up the inner thigh of my pants, her grin widening at what she found hard beneath her foot. "An invitation to explore. There's more of me, Ravenfae Prince. Would you care to discover just how much?"

Fuck, if she asked me to, I'd discover all sorts of things about her skin, her shape, her breath, and what sounds she'd make deep in the throes of pleasure.

This woman did more to me in a few days of our cursed reunion than I'd felt in years. If ever.

But she was a Princess of Riche. I was a Ravenfae Prince. She was cursed in this form until kissed by the one who loved her most, and I had cursed her. I couldn't take advantage of her like this. I couldn't love her most. I put her here. I gave her that curse that had grown so—

"Stop it," she said, startling me from my thoughts. "Stop

thinking about it. Stop trying to figure out if it's right or wrong or any glimpse of the future for either of us." Rising from her chair, the rest of my wool cloak fell, revealing what she meant by more to explore. She had hips. She had a tangible body up to the underside of her ribs. The sharp white satin of her dress adorned in beads and pearls clashed with the creamy softness of her long stockings.

She stood in front of me, finding herself between my legs. I reached out, pulling her closer, rubbing the backs of her thighs. I slid my fingers beneath the hem of her stockings to smooth over her skin.

She leaned toward me, her next damning words a mere whisper for us to hear. "We have now. We have this moment, right now. Will you live it with me?"

I gripped the back of her legs, pulling her even closer. Once again, there I was, a prince looking up at a princess who had the power to be my downfall. "Whatever you want me to do, Seraphine," I promised back, "it's done."

"Touch all of me, Korven. Touch every part of me you can."

She needn't ask me twice.

CHAPTER 18

Seraphine

KORVEN'S HANDS WERE ALL SOFT CARESS AND FIERY burn. His mouth on the skin of my inner thigh was almost too much to bear.

I'd imagined this many times since our reunion. I had romanticized what we could have been. I had given him up years ago, believing myself to be happy there in my own cottage hidden away from the world, only seeking company for my bed when I'd gotten lonely enough.

But there he was with me, kissing his way up to the tiny triangle of silk covering the liquid heat that poured from me in my yearning for his touch. He had easily pulled me to rest my knees on either side of the arms of his chair, spreading his wings out wide behind him to face the hall entry. If anyone passed in the quiet library, they'd see the strange sight of a Ravenfae's wingspan and nothing else.

His strong hands slipped under the roughly cut hem of my wedding gown and pulled at the tiny strings of my undergarments, snapping them against my skin.

Settling himself lower beneath me, his eyes caught mine

in a devilish grin. "How attached are you to these?" He pulled the thin white strings again.

"Not at all—"

Before I could fully finish, he snapped the strings from my body, tossing the thinly sewn undergarment I'd hated since the day my betrothed gifted it to me. Prince Urik would never see them on my body. He'd never rip them off me, either.

As if having the same smug thought, Korven's gaze drifted to everything I had exposed to him. His chest deflated in a carnal rumble, and he slid his hands over my bare backside, squeezing me fully.

"Can I kiss you, Phinie darling?".

I reached out, wishing I could brush my fingers through his hair. "Yes," I answered breathlessly, excitedly, *desperately* because I needed him touching me. I needed his kiss more than he'd ever know and that was the damning truth of it.

He pulled my body to his mouth, offering one kiss against my soft bud, then two. A short moan escaped me and I pushed closer, asking for more.

Another kiss, gentle, restrained, though his hands at my backside told another story. They stroked and squeezed, timed with every kiss he placed across the heat of my skin.

"Korven," I moaned in frustration and dire need of his tongue and hands.

"Tell me," he replied. I felt the heat of his breath as he continued those soft kisses, ending right at the apex of where my pleasure would know no bounds if he would only follow my growing list of demands.

I gulped, my breath releasing quickly from my chest as I listed my requests. "I want you to lick every wet part of me, Korven. I want to come undone over your mouth. I want you to suck and kiss and circle over every inch of what I offer you. I want to reach the peak of a release and try to pull away but you hold me to your mouth to taste all of it—every last drop of the pleasure you give me. I want you to make me scream and cry out in this library so that only you can hear what your clever mouth can do to me. I want you to consume me, Korven. Live this moment with me."

He had paused to listen, but didn't keep me waiting as he licked his lips, lifted me further over his face and answered with a simple, "Done."

CHAPTER 19

Korven

How the fuck I made it back to our room above the inn was beyond me. I didn't remember flying us there. Didn't remember leaving the library. I was still in that hall. I was still under her as she moaned and writhed as I did every little thing she had asked of me.

I could still taste her.

I could still feel the warmth and sweet nectar she gave me and I wanted more. For now, she slept—exhausted, spent, and ravaged by my mouth and hands.

What the fuck was I doing? I asked myself for the hundredth time since I'd met her again and crashed her wedding. *Saved her from her wedding*, I amended.

But I wasn't saving her now. Now, I was indulging, selfishly licking, sucking, thrusting my fingers against her inner core so hard she'd whimpered, pulling away, but I'd kept her there. Just as she'd asked me, I'd held her steady, igniting her release again as she came over my fingers and mouth.

My cock had never been so hard. I'd never abstained like that before. But my Seraphine had asked, and fuck it all, I'd delivered.

I understood my growing obsession with her, but I didn't understand its origins. I had a Goddessdamned job to do, and a mother who would force this Cursebringer life onto my sister in a heartbeat if she didn't believe I could do it.

I wasn't going to let that happen.

Morella wasn't going to live as a Cursebringer. She was young and carefree and would never know our mother's burdens. The same burdens that had led Reshina to suffering and heartbreak, leaving her incapable of love through her own curse.

The line of Cursebringers was a matriarchal one. In over six hundred years my mother hadn't given it up. Goddess knows what happened to her mother before that.

I was determined to end that line with her, and I'd be damned if I let my infatuation with Seraphine Dupont ruin my sister's life.

This was my problem.

This was my curse to help break and move on.

I stroked her leg tangled with mine as she slept away the rest of the afternoon.

I'd live every moment with her I could in these last few days.

And then I'd *keep* living and somehow find the strength to do it without her.

CHAPTER 20

Seraphine

WHEN I WOKE, THE SKY ON THE OTHER SIDE OF THE diamond paned window was black and stars twinkled with a silver streak of moonlight across the bed and floor.

Korven was gone and in the absence of his warm body I'd fallen into, utterly exhausted and sated, I was bundled in blankets.

I pushed up from the bed, calling his name—bleary, and a bit disoriented. I didn't need food or water to live in this state apparently, but I felt the lack of it in the way my limbs felt so suddenly heavy.

I yawned and closed my eyes, bringing myself back to focus.

Yes, I had ground myself over Korven's mouth and hands in the library.

No, I didn't regret it.

Yes, I was falling harder than ever for him.

No, I didn't expect any returned feelings.

The Duke of Riche was kind. Interesting. The perfect man on paper. And by the way my body was returning so rapidly, he was also the best option we had to break this spell.

We had six more days. I'd have sent him directly to Castle Havenshire that night if I thought Prince Urik would let him in.

Goddess be, I didn't want to know the condition of my body in that castle or what had been done to it. Fiola said she'd keep me safe there, but I had little trust in the Prince of Havenshire.

So, I had one chance with Arthur. I would be honest with him at our next meeting and explain that my heart could not be his, but if he would break this curse, I would be so grateful. It would have to be a strong man who felt he could love me most, but would be denied anything in return from the woman he saved.

I untangled myself from the sheets and picked up the note on the table, written in Korven's messy scrawl.

GONE TO THE BATH IN THE CELLAR TO SOAK. IF YOU'RE READING THIS BEFORE I RETURN, THEN YES, I AM A SHITTY CHAPERONE, AND WILL MAKE IT UP TO YOU.

YES, IN THAT WAY IF YOU'LL LET ME.

—K

I chuckled to myself and let the note fall to the table.
The note fell to the table.
From my hands.
I'd been so worked up on what I was feeling and what had happened, it took me all of two minutes to realize I had *hands.*

I still only had a waist to the base of my breasts, but some-time during that sleep, once again, more of me had become tangible and real. I had fingers, wrists, and forearms. That's where it ended. Floating parts of my arm waved out in front of my face and I shook.

We could really do this.

The curse could fully break and we were getting close, so very close.

I needed to spend more time with Arthur. I needed him to understand and agree to help. Now I could.

With hands, we didn't need Korven to interpret any longer.

I could write.

IT WASN'T EASY WRAPPING KORVEN'S CLOAK AROUND half of my body, holding it to me in such a way that it appeared that a Wildefae or child was pushing through the busy tavern instead of the waist and legs of an adult woman.

I managed to fold the wool to look as if I was smaller than a human with a shadowy hood to hide my face. I received some long-lingered looks, but brushed through the dinner crowd, past the usual drunks, and made it to the cellar door. I waited in the shadowy corner for it to unlock and the maid to leave with what was hopefully the last bucket of hot water she'd delivered.

From what I remembered on my first night when I fell through the booth and saw the cellar below, there was one bath sunken into the tiled floor, surrounded by boxes and barrels of ale.

I slipped through the door as the maid left, descending the stone steps quietly and coming to another door.

I knocked three times to hear Korven shout back, "I need nothing more, please go!"

I leaned in and called, "It's Seraphine. I'm sorry to interrupt you, but I thought you might like to know that—"

The door flew open to reveal a dripping wet Ravenfae Prince holding a towel bundled at his waist.

Eyes wide, I took all of him in. Candles were lit behind him, creating a halo effect around his black feathers and his dripping black hair. Rivulets of water slid down his muscled chest, slipping along his skin to the towel he held over his hips. I followed the beads of water with my eyes, wishing I had a tongue to follow them with instead.

"How in the name of Revelry did you get down here without being seen as half a woman?"

I reluctantly looked away from the deep V and black hair that led from his navel downward. "Huh?" I uttered.

"Phinie," he sighed, then reached behind me, coaxing me through the door and locking it with a loud click.

I looked around to see a full bath buried in the ground, elliptical in shape with candles lit around the edge. This room was definitely also a supply room because barrels of ale and bags of flour and sugar were stacked and slumped against the walls. Even a crate of carrots sat near the door.

"What were you doing coming down here?" he scolded. "You could have been seen and then we'd have some explaining to do."

He shuffled away from the door, walking to the edge of the tub and dropping his towel.

Goddess be damned, his wings hid anything I'd wanted to see from his backside. The depths of the bath hid everything in the front, except for his chiseled chest, and I'd seen plenty of that. He swiveled to the edge of the water and motioned for me to come to him. "You might as well get in. Come here and

I'll help you with..." he trailed off, actually noticing me for the first time.

I dropped his cloak and waved.

"When, Phinie darling, did you get hands?"

"I woke up with them."

A grin broke across his face. "I suppose it's one reason to thank the duke," he muttered. "By all means, please join me in a soak. I'm sorry you woke up alone. My shoulders ached a bit from...ah...our earlier festivities and I needed a moment to relax."

"I can go, if you prefer to be alone. I just wanted you to see—"

He flicked water my way from the tub, splashing over my legs. "You're already wet now, you might as well get in."

I gasped with a laugh, teasing, "How dare you get me wet, Your Highness."

"Tell me just how wet you are, Seraphine."

My lower belly knotted, anticipation rising and overtaking my senses.

There he was, the only man I'd ever really cared deeply for, naked in a steaming bath surrounded by candlelight.

If these were to be my last few days—as they might be—I wanted to spend them touching his skin, his wings, his mouth. I would take what earthly delights he'd let me, damn what that meant for the future. I was possibly a dying woman, though evidence of myself returning would say otherwise, and I would live the next few days as well as I could.

"Seraphine."

My eyes shot from his chest to his face and I smiled at his raw, hungry gaze.

Oh, yes. He wanted to live with me just as badly.

"If I'm to join you, I need a knife," I said sweetly, padding in my stocking feet to his clothing.

He laughed and glided through the water to the other side of the tub, watching me rifle through his things. "No need for violence. I won't touch anything you don't want me to. I won't even look." He covered his eyes with his hands, peeking through two of his fingers.

Finding what I needed, I shook my head in a laugh. "I'd prefer you look."

He dropped his hands and watched as I cut away the raw hem of my gown. I had no undergarments underneath, no shield against any look he gave me as I pulled and cut away swaths of material. I cut the threads attaching the skirt of the gown to the corseted top. When I'd shredded enough away, I yanked at the threads, dropping what was left of the skirt of my gown to the cellar floor, flicking it to a corner with my foot.

His mouth parted and his eyes drifted slowly up my body, all the way to my face, ethereal and untouchable. Unkissable.

I tossed his knife back toward his boot and took two steps to the edge of the inlaid tub, just as he moved across the water to meet me there.

He rose, revealing just how much I affected him, too, and lifted his hands from the water. "May I?" he asked, gesturing to the stockings he'd made resting at my mid thigh.

I nodded and he began the slow, teasing work of rolling each down my leg. His wet fingers slid beneath the hem, his mouth leaving light kisses down my thighs and knees. He lifted each foot at the final roll, laying my stockings to the side as gently as he'd pulled them down.

His fingers trailed across my skin, his mouth hot near the top of my thighs, and I felt the chill and excitement that surged through my veins at what pleasures the night held for us both.

"Are you cold, Phinie darling?"

I nodded and raked my fingers through his black locks. He closed his eyes, tilting his head back with a smile.

"Keep me warm, Korven," I murmured low in the candlelit cellar.

"Done."

He kissed me once, twice, his lips once again gentle and soft between my legs. He grabbed my hips and pressed me down to sit at the edge of the tub. My long legs slid over his shoulders, resting across the vast expanse of his black wings. I admired how they reflected in the candlelight, taking in their beauty as Korven began to abide by his promise.

Warm and wet, I pushed myself up against his mouth, my hands running through his hair, gripping him tightly as his tongue swept over every pleasurable surface of my body. He explored everything, everywhere, and I gasped when his fingers joined his tongue in pursuit of what ways he could make me moan, make me cry out in delighted surprise. But it wasn't until I called his name, harsh, urgent, his mouth sucking, his fingers pulsing, that he looked up at me with that smoldering grin I'd now seen enough of to know I'd never be rid of it.

All the days of my life I had left to live, regardless of how few, I'd remember his face laced with raw hunger in the way he watched me come undone. Our eyes locked as I called his name again in the night, slick over his fingers and face, marking him with the scent and taste of me.

As I caught my breath, gulping down heaps of air, he kissed my thighs gently, once again with his promise. "Whatever you want me to do, Phinie darling, it's done."

"I—" I swallowed hard, ready again to take what I wanted. "I want you inside me, Korven. I want you inside me every last night of this fucking curse."

His cock thrust hard, slipping into me with ease the

moment the last word left my mouth. I whimpered, holding onto his shoulders for dear life as he pleased us both without hesitation—without the slow down of a lesser man who could tire with ease.

No, not this Ravenfae Prince.

He fucked, and groaned, and gripped my hips like a dying man, starved and bereft of anything so delectable as me. I'd done this to him. I'd gotten under his skin as my own formed along my forearm, revealing elbows, up the length of my biceps, revealing shoulders, across my ribs to the base of my breasts.

His wild fucking slowed, both of us attempting to catch our breath, my body pulsing, needy and ready for more. His lips met my shoulder, his tongue sliding across my skin. "There's more of you." He bit the top of my shoulder and stared into my eyes face-to-face, no running from the heat of his gaze as the head of his cock withdrew from me and slipped in to the hilt once more. "Why is there more of you, Seraphine?"

The peak of my nipples ached, irritated against the stiff corset of my dress. He noticed at the same time I did. My breasts were full, heaping over the top of the ridiculously sized bow, heaving from the breath leaving me so quickly.

"I-I don't know," I stumbled, digging my nails into the skin of his back, asking for more, needing more.

"You do know," he said in a deep rumble, withdrawing from me completely, catching the pained cry when his hands left my hips only to yank down the top of my corset, pulling the taut peak of my nipple into his mouth.

"Please," I begged, "get this off me."

In a growl, he had me turned, flipping me to my stomach, halfway in the bath, half across the tiled cellar floor. His knee separated my legs and his hard cock, slick from me, was filling my body again, rising a desperate moan from my lips.

He pulled the back of my corset strings, bringing me upright, his teeth again at my shoulder, my breasts bare as he held my back to his chest.

"You ask me to free you fully from this cage."

"Yes!" I cried, touching myself and lifting a leg to the edge of the tub.

"I require something in return," he purred between strokes over the swell of my breasts.

"Anything," I answered in a raptured daze, ready to lay down whatever he wanted so we could get back to that mindless place of pleasure.

I heard the grin in his voice as he pressed me back down, pulling on the knot, flicking the first bundle of strings loose from the corset. "Tell me the curse saved you."

I gasped, grunting as another string flew loose and he pushed himself deeper.

"Tell me I saved you."

Another string. The tight bodice began to loosen, and I could finally take a real breath.

"Tell me your body returns for me."

Thrust.

"I see no duke here."

Withdraw.

"Only a prince."

Thrust.

I cried out in an urgent unrest. I'd tell him. I'd give him the words he wanted and more, Goddess only knew what would spill from my lips as long as he stayed inside me.

The vice across my torso fell limp and loose as he pulled out the last of the strings, tossing them across the room at the same time I pulled away from the boned corset, throwing it hard against the wall.

"Tell me—"

He stopped mid demand for the payment of this act of freedom. His fingers trailed down my spine and I stiffened.

I knew what he touched.

In my lust and longing for him to fill me, I'd forgotten.

In my pleasure-addled mind, I'd become negligent in what I'd hidden from anyone for so, so long.

A chill swept through what parts of me it could as he stepped back, slipping out of me completely, still holding me in place, still tracing my back.

"What is this, Seraphine?"

Him.

It was him and he knew it.

It was a lonely young woman holding onto and chasing that one glimpse of care she'd felt fifteen years before.

His fingers traced the lines of my feather tattoo, sweeping across the downy barbs, the hollow shaft, inked in perfection along the spine of my back in remembrance and reminder of what I had found once and never again.

"Phinie..." he murmured and I turned, backing as far away from him as I could.

He stopped me before I could climb out and cover myself in the shame I felt at having inked my skin with his memory.

"It's nothing," I said, breathless.

His fingers pressed into my bare hips, locking me in place. "It's not nothing. Why is one of my feathers inked across your back?"

"I just liked it," I lied.

He jostled me, calling me on it instantly. "Bullshit. You had this done for a reason. Goddess knows where you even found someone in Moonstone Wood to—"

"He was visiting. From Songbird Cove. Said he tattooed all the pirates there and was traveling Revelry, adding art to his trade." I gulped, wild eyed in his piercing gaze. I rambled on. "Said he'd ink me for a few jars of salve that heals inked skin quickly. I didn't know what to get, so, I got this." I reached behind my back, tracing what I knew to be the point of the feather.

"Seraphine…" he breathed, leaning close, close enough to kiss if he'd been able to touch my lips.

"Don't. Don't pity me. Don't touch me in sadness for something that is mine. It was a choice I made. It means nothing."

His fingers dug into my skin harder. "I don't believe you."

"I don't care if you believe me."

"You do." His hand reached up to my face, unable to catch the tear that fell.

Goddessdamn him. Goddessdamn how quickly, in the pursuit of pleasure, I'd forgotten what he'd find when he tore the last remaining piece of my wedding gown from my skin.

"It's just a feather. I like feathers."

"It's not just a feather."

"It is! Stop trying to make it about you!"

"It is about me."

"I did not tattoo myself for you, Korven."

"You did. That's the same feather I gave you."

I scoffed, rolling my eyes and trying to squirm away from his hold on me. "How would you know?"

"It has the notch cut out on the barbs. The exact same feather I left for you that day under the tree when you didn't fucking come back."

He stunned me into silence. His fingers slid up my sides, his thumbs caressing the pebbled skin under my breasts.

"H-how would you remember that exact feather?"

"I left you the first feather of mine you'd ever touched. After you woke up from sleeping in my arms one day, you smiled and reached out to touch one. It was that one. As imperfect as it was, you chose that one. So don't tell me this isn't personal."

I couldn't deny just how personal it was any longer.

He knew.

I knew.

He knew I knew he knew.

"When did you get it?" he asked softly.

"Five years ago."

He shook me, his voice rising. "You've been missing me for five years?"

"I've been missing you most of my life!" I spat, mirroring his tone. "There. I said it, and I hope you're happy. I hope you think of it often if we're still alive in a week, and I hope memories of me haunt your dreams just as they've haunted mine. You want me to say I wanted this? I'm thankful for *this*?" I gestured to his body and he stilled his hands on my skin. "I've lived more true to myself in the past *four days* than I have in the past ten years, and, yes, I am glad. I am glad that it was you with the curse. That you have been forced to break it with me. I'm glad I have the courage to take exactly what I want for the first time in my life. I won't be summoned again to visit the Forestfae court and end up bringing home a stranger. If this curse breaks, I will live. I will love. Because I deserve it. And yes, I tattooed the feather I lost onto my skin and with every prick of every needle, I remembered you. Every fucking one."

Something broke on his face. Lust? Anger? A confirmation of knowing what his memory had done to me over the years?

He spoke softly, firming his grip and keeping me in place

with one hand, trailing up the new skin of my reappearing neck with the other. "You love me, Phinie darling?"

I couldn't do it. As cowardly as it made me, I wasn't ready to confess my answer. "I remembered you," I said in partial truth. "I always remembered you."

He nodded, his jaw ticking. "I will help you break this curse."

Anger rushed to the surface and my chest heaved in frustration. "I doubt I *need* you further. I can manage to get to the library on my own now."

He caressed my neck. "No fucking chance. I'm sticking to your ass like the freckle I just found there."

"I don't want you on my ass."

He chuckled in that soft sultry way, leaning in to whisper, "Then why the fuck are your legs still wrapped around me?"

I dropped them immediately, but he was ready, catching me under the knees. He tsked, shaking his head. "You want to live, Seraphine? Then let's live." His kiss was back on the swell of my breasts, the hollow of my throat, and I found myself pushing into the hard length of him, my body begging to finish what we'd started.

A guttural growl came deep from his chest and he picked me up, settling my clit over the head of his cock, a question ready in his next breath. "Do you want me to put you down, Phinie darling?"

I squirmed, wrapping my legs tighter around him. "Put me down where?"

His chest rumbled in response. He cupped my ass with one hand and trailed down my tattoo with the other. "Whatever you want me to do, it's done."

I reached down between us, my hand following the dark hair of his stomach, over the hard planes of muscle, reaching, stroking. Our eyes locked as I touched him. Desire filled his eyes, deep and haunting. I couldn't look away. Neither could he from me as I wrapped my hand around the base of his cock, lining myself up to slide down on top of him.

He sucked air between his teeth as he filled me and I began again to ease myself up and down, returning to that ache that begged to be released.

"No confessions, no commitment," I said, repeating what I'd told the duke just hours before. "Just live these last days with me. Fuck me in every one."

His fingers pressed harder to my tattoo and he settled me back on the edge of the tub, laying me down and lifting each of my ankles up to his shoulders. He kissed the pad of my foot before beginning again where we'd left off, his breath hot on my skin. "Done, my darling Seraphine."

CHAPTER 21

Korven

WHAT COULD BE SO GODDESSDAMNED FUNNY?

It certainly couldn't be anything the Duke of Fucking Riche was saying. Or…writing, really.

The two of them—holed up in a back hall of the library.

Writing little notes to each other.

I raked my fingers against my scalp again and my hair fell across my face. I couldn't stand it. I *wouldn't* stand it much longer. Their hour was almost up, but since I was the time-keeper, I could decide how long an hour really was.

Her laugh chimed again, and though the duke couldn't hear it, I didn't doubt the fucker could see it in her body. The way she shook and adjusted herself. Maybe brought her hand to her mouth in habit.

I had watched their interaction for the first ten minutes or so before I knew I should leave to the end of the hall before the bastard left with a black eye and broken ribs.

Jealousy raked her claws in my skin, and I couldn't get away. The thing was, I'd never experienced it before Seraphine. I refused to explore if that was a good or bad thing.

I rolled my eyes and pulled my hair back again, remembering I wasn't going down this road.

The duke chuckled and I heard the faint scratch of one of their quills.

I needed to get out of there.

My feet started moving, confident she was safe enough for me to walk a few halls down. Maybe I could pick up a few books for us to take back to our room to read after we'd fucked until we couldn't take any more.

My hands trailed along the bookcases of each open hall I passed, slipping over the smooth carvings of ornate swirls and flourishes. I entered the empty hall of natural history. Two whole halls away from Seraphine and the Prick.

Plants.

Animals.

Bones of things I couldn't name.

The reference book for this section was as thick as my palm was wide, and when I flipped it open, a cloud of dust spread around me. Coughing, I searched for the books I guessed would interest Seraphine most.

Top shelf. Seven hundreds.

A ladder on rollers shadowed the corner of the hall, probably collecting cobwebs and more dust than the reference tome.

I flew.

My wings, unaccustomed to spreading in such tight quarters, knocked several books to the floor below, and it took a moment to adjust my wingspan, searching for the seven hundreds. The great whoosh of my wings was bound to attract unwanted attention from the scribes, so I grabbed a few hefty volumes and began my descent.

Slightly off-kilter, I flew sideways to the entrance of the

hall, exposed to the main floor for a brief moment, locking eyes with one of Prince Urik's guards.

Though he wore plain clothing, I recognized him instantly. I had a knack for faces and his was gruff and blotched with a nose so crooked, I'd wager it had been broken multiple times.

He fled and hurried out the great front doors. I tucked my books under my arm and rushed across the aisle, shifting into a raven to glide over the balcony railing and back to Ravenfae, just seconds behind him when a scribe stepped into my path.

"Can I help you with those, Sir?"

"Move," I snapped, stepping around him.

He grabbed the thick books from under my arm, spinning with surprising sprightliness. "You will not be taking these outside of this library without the proper paperwork."

He was brave, I'd give him that. It wasn't just anyone who would stop a Ravenfae from taking anything out of anywhere.

"Fine," I growled, nudging him out of my way as I raced up the few steps, bursting out of the doors.

The waning sun blinded me to the west, and I peered out into the street, searching for the guard I knew belonged to Seraphine's betrothed.

So, the Prince of Havenshire had sent a spy.

As I shifted and flew toward the sun, searching below for any sign of him, I worried about Seraphine's body back at the castle. If he touched her...if he did anything to harm a hair on her head...

I landed on the bannister of the belfry at the Altar of the Veiled Ones. Shifting back, I cursed, still scanning the streets with no clue as to where the guard had gone.

No matter. We still had a few days left and I knew the general area where I could find him, beat the shit out of him, and get some answers.

Seraphine was not marrying the Prince of Havenshire.

She wasn't marrying the asshole Duke of Riche, either.

And she wasn't marrying me.

That truth sat hard in my chest.

But I wouldn't dwell. I would live the days we had left. Phinie and I had a date planned in the marketplace, and the duke's time was up.

I spread my wings, ready to shift back to raven and tell the duke to get the fuck out when I froze in place, immobilized mid leap from the tower.

A voice echoed between the stone walls and off the copper bell, ringing in my head where I did not want to hear.

"Korven," it drawled. I would say with love, but I didn't think her capable.

I caught myself as she lifted the spell holding me in place and drifted back into the tower, taking a massive breath, readying myself for the conversation to come.

"Hello, Mother," I greeted, hands shoved in my pockets, back leaning across the cold stone. "What brings the Ravenfae Goddess to Havenshire?"

CHAPTER 22

Seraphine

ARTHUR'S PENMANSHIP LOOPED AND SWIRLED, written with utmost care—just as I would expect from a Duke of Riche. The quill scratched across the open notebook he'd brought with him, and I studied his face.

He was certainly a good looking man. Golden hair. Golden skin that made me wonder how much time he spent outdoors when he claimed to spend most of it inside. That scar down his cheek did him wonders, and I was growing more curious to know how he'd gotten it.

What hangs at a man's thigh and is used to poke at holes that have been poked many times before?

I laughed, though he couldn't hear me. He smiled with a sly grin, and I took the quill from his hand.

I actually knew this one.

> *A Key.*

"Ah, you've heard this one before. Two out of eight isn't so bad." He leaned back in his chair, stretching his legs.

I quickly wrote,

> *Two out of eight is terrible.*

Reading my words, he chuckled, rubbing his eyes and covering a yawn.

> *Do you tire? I could call for Kor*

"No, no," he interrupted my quick scrawl. "I apologize, Your Highness. I've had a few long nights."

Arthur was kind and intelligent. Well-read in books and naughty jokes. He was a duke and everything I should have wanted if I had been raised as the Princess of Riche.

I tapped my foot while watching him as he cocked his head and studied the spines of the books in the hall. There was a tension in his shoulders—a subtle way he tried to hide whatever was bothering him.

I liked Arthur's company. I could see a life where we were friends, exchanging book recommendations and laughing over our lewd humor. But I could not see myself loving or settling down somewhere with this man.

I picked up the quill and began to write again.

> *Would you like to tell me about your long nights? Something is bothering you.*

He leaned in and read my words. He shook his head. "I wouldn't let my concerns weigh over your head."

I picked up the quill again.

You know of mine. Though we are strangers in a strange circumstance, you have a listening ear.

I paused, then added,

I'm of more use than trying out all your naughty jokes, Duke of Riche.

His body shook in a chuckle and he rubbed his chest, standing and walking along the shelves, pulling a book to rifle through.

"My mother will be dead in days," he began. "I have come to accept this. What hope I had of her return to health is fading with each night that passes."

I quickly wrote a reply.

I am truly sorry. Is there anything I can do to help besides listen?

He read my words, staring too long at the page. A minute went by. I continued,

Perhaps my birth parents can find some way to be of help? I'm sure they have the best resources money can buy.

"It is not resources she needs." He was staring now. Staring at where my eyes should be. "She needs a Goddess blessing and—"

I know the Forestfae Goddess of the Veil! I'm sure she could help you save your mother.

He leaned against the desk, a rumble leaving his chest. "I have...procured a way to possibly save her life. It isn't...guaranteed." His hands bent, fingers scratching in the wood. "Never mind it all, Princess. She will live or die. Life goes on, doesn't it?"

I frowned.

You care immensely for your mother. It is perfectly normal to grieve her possible passing before she goes.

"Seraphine," he whispered harshly. "You don't understand. And I cannot—"

"Your time is up," Korven called, practically flying across the long aisle, his wingspan flaring.

Arthur stood straight, a small grin across his mouth. "You're late by my timing, Prince Korven. And I half expected you to burst in here early. What kept you?"

"None of your fucking business," he snapped, holding a hand out to me, his harsh tone calming as he asked, "Are you ready?"

I nodded, my body instantly drawn to the winged Raven-fae, dark and broody, jealous and possessive. The man who had woken me this morning with his mouth across my belly, his teeth nipping at my hip.

I took up the quill one more time.

It was good to see you again, Arthur. Will you meet me here tomorrow?

He cleared his throat, plastering a soft smile on his face. "Alas, I cannot, Princess Seraphine. I am to travel once more to our castle in Heartstone Wood and will be away for a few days."

My stomach fell. In five days the curse breaker was due to kiss me and end this spell. I began to write again, but Korven beat me to it.

"You fucking bastard. You know she has just days left and you lead us on with the pretense of breaking—"

"I'll do it," he stated, then turned back to me. "I'll be there, Seraphine. Before the moon is full, I will find you in the tallest tower." He huffed a laugh and reached for my hand. "I'll kiss your lips and you will be done with this curse. No commitments. No confessions. I believe I can give you what you need." He swallowed hard, squeezing my hand. "I'd be happy to give you your life back."

"Go now. Go right fucking now," Korven moved around the desk, grabbing my other hand, pulling me toward him. "Why wait? You've made up your mind. If you tell Urik why you're there—hell, we'll escort you and explain everything."

"I cannot go. My carriage is already waiting outside, and I am overdue to travel to my mother and see her one last time. I don't...I don't know if I'll make it in time even as it is." He bowed to me, taking my hand to kiss softly.

Korven tensed, squeezing my fingers.

"I will be there. Before the Cursed Moon is full in the sky. This is my promise to you."

I nodded, squeezing his fingers in my reply. He gave one last look my way before leaving the hall swiftly.

I beamed at Korven. "He'll do it. He's going to break the curse!" I wrapped my arms around his neck. "I believe him. His mother will pass very soon, and I can only imagine he needs to say his goodbye. We will be free."

He pulled me to his chest, cupping the base of my neck. "You're willing to bet your life on his promises?"

I breathed deep. "Yes. And yours. I believe him, Korven. Please trust me in this. We don't have time to find another." I pressed myself against him and he hummed low. "We have these next few days to live. No appointments with dukes, no long list of pompous gentlemen."

His fingers trailed over my spine, across the back of the barmaid's dress he'd swiped from the line early this morning. "There's one more thing to do then, before we live them together."

It was my turn to hum, pressing my breasts harder against him and finding my way up his shirt. "And what's that, Ravenfae Prince?"

He caught my hand along the planes of muscle across his torso, pulling it back out and kissing the tips of my fingers. "It's time we find you a dress you belong in."

KORVEN HELD MY HAND AS WE WALKED THROUGH Thornhill's streets, stopping with me at stalls and storefronts, never satisfied enough with a dress color or drape. I wore his cloak and he positioned it in such a way that the hood fell over my neck to appear as if he walked with a mysterious figure and not a headless woman. It was the only part of me that had not yet solidified, and thankfully, Thornhill wasn't exactly a hub of faekind that could see me partially returned. The Ravenfae Prince was avoided throughout the streets and it took me all of five minutes to see that he preferred it that way.

Each gown we looked over was too bright, too rough— never good enough for his Seraphine, he'd told me over and over again.

The sun left its last sliver of gold glowing across the cobblestones, and I could have stayed there, my hand in my possessive prince's fingers, walking the market stores and stalls in search of something to drape across my body. If I had an endless day, it might be this, holding hands through the streets with the man I couldn't bear to think of leaving.

"Are you certain I even need a gown?" I asked him as he swept his hand over the material of a pale blue silk, bent in a crouch to inspect the hem. "I don't need to wear anything at all for the next few days."

His wings ruffled and he gave me a slow head turn with a devouring look.

I giggled, pulling at my drab brown skirts. "I find that most material is a bit irritating on my skin. I prefer nothing but soft stockings to warm my legs and a fae prince between them."

He grabbed a handful of my dress, pulling me closer to where he bent, focusing back on his assessment. "One more teasing remark from you, and I'll be under these skirts before you can say—"

"My Prince! I've found it!" The little old man who owned the small boutique came rushing toward us, a gown of bright pink silk draped over his outstretched arms. Korven rose and murmured his reply, inspecting the material.

I sighed and continued looking around, not really caring much for whatever Korven found to drape across my body. I'd been forced into one too many gowns in my life to have a love of fashion. I'd meant what I'd said. I'd rather wear soft blankets and sheets than be draped in yards of silk.

I trailed my fingers over the gowns on display, lovely, intricate, loud. I couldn't see myself in any of them. But I wanted to find something Korven would admire and force him to catch his breath like I did every Goddessdamn time I saw him.

I found it there, nestled behind two beaded gowns in dark jewel tones. It had been shoved behind them as if forgotten or too plain for any customer to look over twice.

It was perfect for me. Soft lilac with draped panels of a blush pink falling over the cinched waist, the gown puddled at the skirts with a wide hem and not a single bead or crystal embellishment to be found. And no bows in sight. The top was delicately folded again and again in long lines across the unstructured bodice with thin straps to hold it in place.

I carefully unhooked it from the hanger and carried it to a private dressing room in the corner. I swept the curtain aside and stepped through, hearing the muffled voices of Korven and the shopkeep discussing the materials he had on hand.

I slipped out of the cloak and my stolen dress, keeping my stockings on. I adored them and would wear them as long as I could.

I stepped into the gown, sliding the soft fabric up over my hips. I hadn't realized the back was open, a few strings tying low just above my backside. I turned and looked at my back in the mirror, smiling at newly golden hair reaching almost to my black feather tattoo.

"There's more of you, Phinie darling."

I gasped, heat coursing through me as he stepped all the way into the dressing room, closing the curtain behind him.

I finished the tie and stepped back, pulling lightly at the layers of soft, silky material, letting it fall along my legs in a gauzy drape.

A short exhale left him and his nostrils flared as he took all of me in. His dark eyes studied me from bottom to top, stopping at the golden curls draped around my shoulders. They ended at my neck, my head still under Fiola's exception to the curse.

He spoke slowly. "Why is there more of you?"

Ignoring his question, I spun with my back on display, the tattoo we both knew was for him bold and black down my spine. "Do you like it? I think it's perfect for me."

"It is," he started, taking the few steps left between us, wings outright and brushing the sides of the walls. His face spoke of promise, of confession—everything we said we wouldn't give each other hung there as he pulled me close.

I couldn't hear it. Even if he wanted to confess whatever pulled at his lips in that shadowy room, I didn't want to know.

In a few days we'd be dead or he'd be gone.

I wouldn't spend the next few days wondering why, grieving the broken loss of him in my bed before he actually left it.

"Seraphine, I—"

"No," I whispered, brushing my fingers across his lips. "Just live with me. Please."

He pulled a pouch of gold from his pocket. The marks clinked as he tossed them to the floor. He picked me up, draped across his arms like a broken princess and walked out the door, our eyes locked, soaring above a world where we would never be together longer than the length of a curse.

CHAPTER 23

Korven

I HAD MEMORIZED THE BLACK LINES OF HER TATTOO two days into discovering it there, inked across her back so quietly. But the message was loud.

The message she left for me to never find was deafening and ringing in my ears as I sucked on her clit, driving a moan from her chest while she squeezed my cock in her hands.

I couldn't get over it.

She'd marked herself with me and the memory of us sharing warm days as children meeting under a Goddess-damned tree.

How could a fleeting childhood friendship have marked her inside and out?

In the two days after she'd found the gown that was made for her, she hadn't worn it again. It fell across a chair, discarded and lovely, but never across her body because her body had been across mine.

I grabbed her ass, filling my mouth with her as she rode my tongue. Her taste, her warmth, her skin and groans replaced any necessity of living in the last few days of hazy pleasure-fueled hours.

We lived and fucked and lived some more while fucking, and if I could, I'd have spent these days over and over again for a lifetime. Indulging. Luxuriating. Basking in the scent and sounds we made together that had never existed before.

Her hands stroked my dick, forever hard in this bed, always ready. She gripped me, gasping for breath after I slid two fingers into her and curled, finding that place that always made her body tremble.

I'd called her mine in this bed more times than I could count, and each time, I knew it wasn't true. I couldn't keep her.

Keeping her would mean I'd failed my sister and that was something else I couldn't do.

Her hands were around my shaft, stroking before she lifted her body above my face, sliding her own fingers into her entrance, wetting them and then spreading her succulent heat across the head of my cock.

"Are you fucking kidding me," I growled, not in question, but in the scorching disbelief of how affected I was at every fucking little thing she did.

I flipped her instantly, one of her stockinged legs pressed at my chest and over my shoulder, the other I held down, squeezing her thigh to the bed as my cock drove into her in the fucking she deserved for that move.

I nipped at her neck through her moans, willing to give up every thrust deep into her if it just meant her lips would return, and I could kiss her.

And there it was.

What I wanted most was to kiss Seraphine Dupont.

In my lust-fueled pounding, I admitted that I had half a mind to fly to the top tower of Castle Havenshire right then, find her body draped in that stupid fucking wedding gown, kiss her lips, and wake her the fuck up so she could really be mine.

It was more than wanting her body. I wanted to know all her ins and outs. Why she sometimes stumbled on her words. Why she studied me so quietly when she thought I didn't notice. Why she was so Goddessdamned *nice* and wanted to continue making her jars of ointments instead of living richly as the Princess of Riche. Why she held onto the memory of us so hard, choosing to let us settle into her skin instead of moving on.

She could have moved on.

I didn't doubt she could have taken any of those Forestfae to her bed.

I wouldn't be surprised if they had lined up at her door.

But she'd chosen a quiet life.

I wanted to *be* a part of her quiet life.

Without a word, she pushed me over, sweeping her body in flawless movement to ride my cock her own way, taking the lead, taking what she wanted from me.

Her skin flushed across her chest as she leaned back, my dick hitting just where she liked. I circled her clit with my thumb and watched in fucking awe of this woman forced back into my life, and now I didn't think I could let her go again.

Fuck leaving her a feather.

I pressed harder, enhancing her cries of release as she rode me wildly.

I'd leave her with more reasons to ink me across her skin.

I'd leave her knowing she meant something to me.

I'd leave her?

No.

With each passing hour, I knew I was beyond the point of leaving.

CHAPTER 24

Seraphine

"MOONSTONE HOLDS MEDICINAL PROPERTIES YET TO be fully discovered. It is propagated in Moonstone Wood, a forest of Revelry inhabited by the private and secluded Forestfae with a populace unknown in true numbers, ruled over by Fiola, a Goddess of the Veil."

Korven paused his reading, tapping my breast bone where he held my back to his chest. "Is this true? Are the Forestfae so private about their population?"

I nodded, stroking the back of his hand, enveloped in the warmth of his black feathers that wrapped around my bare skin. "What would you guess their numbers are?"

He set the heavy volume on the floor and tossed his reading glasses on top. I shifted my head to see his face. He pressed harder between my breasts, deterring any further movement.

"Ten thousand."

"You're off by a few thousand at least."

"Less or more?"

I hummed, slipping from his hold to turn, pressing my

chest against his, my finger sliding down the length of his wing. "Wouldn't you like to know?"

His eyes narrowed and his chest rumbled. "More secrets you're keeping from me, Phinie darling?"

"As if you don't keep secrets yourself, Ravenfae Prince of the Brackish Wood."

He hummed in reply, cupping my ass and pressing himself to my stomach. "Suppose I haven't explored you enough." He sat upright, taking me with and pulling my legs around his hips. He lifted one of my breasts and peeked underneath. "If I find a number in the thousands tattooed on your skin, I'll know what it means."

He continued to search, caressing my skin, kissing everywhere he touched as I laughed, falling into him. "Do you not tire, my Prince?"

"I need no rest or sustenance. You are all I need."

A well-timed grumble from his stomach had both of us snickering.

I slipped out of his grasp, maneuvering around his attempt to pull me back in. I stood out of his reach, examining the food he'd spent less than ten minutes buying at the market.

"Let's see," I began, pulling each item out of the sack. "We have two rolls of bread, a single beef pasty now crumbling with gravy everywhere—"

He prowled on his knees across the bed, black wings spread wide like a predator ready to pounce. I held up a hand. "Not now. You need to eat something before you pass out."

"Oh, I'll eat something alright."

I ignored him, suppressing a smile that would only encourage him further. "And last but not least, a carton of bramble berries. My favorite—but—ugh! They're mostly crushed, Korven!"

I wiped the bright pink juice across my stomach, bits of berry flesh spread across my skin. His eyes lowered and his mouth parted.

I scoffed, determined to get my way. "Don't look at me like that. You're going to eat. Now."

He stepped out of the bed, rising tall and every bit a royal Ravenfae before me. "Is that a command?"

"Yes. Promise me you'll eat something. I haven't seen you eat in two days."

He lowered slowly, bending to his knees with hands at my waist before his tongue replaced them. His mouth slid across my stomach, taking care of the berry remnants I had wiped there.

"I promise I'll eat, my darling." He kissed my skin, pulling me closer. "Now get back in bed. You're going to be my plate."

I WOKE IN A GASP, MY MIND SCRAMBLING TO FIND solid ground. I had dreamed the Cursed Moon was already full. We were too late and my body faded away. Arthur hadn't shown to kiss my lips in the tower of Havenshire Castle.

I scrambled to the window, shielding my eyes at a setting sun, still another hour or two before the moon would have a chance to rise and another few hours after that until its peak in the night sky.

Tonight was the Cursed Moon and our last day had been spent just as the previous three. Korven read aloud from the book he swiped from the library. I laid on his chest to listen, occasionally feeding him with my fingers, which tended to wander along with his and there we were, at it again.

We had fucked like each time was the last, and except for a quick trip to scrub the bramble berry juice from our bodies and exchange our sheets, we hadn't left the room at the top of the Rose and Briar for days.

But hours before Arthur was due to arrive at the castle and break the curse, Korven was gone. I pulled myself from the sheets, darting to the small table littered with smushed bramble berries. He'd left another note, this one with drying ink.

IF YOU WAKE BEFORE I RETURN, YOU MAY PUNISH ME WITH ANY METHOD YOU SEE FIT.

LOOKING FORWARD TO IT.

—K

My heart fell a little, fearing what reason he had to leave just hours before we would be parted.

We hadn't spoken about it.

We hadn't talked about what would happen next, but I knew one thing for certain; I was not going to marry Prince Urik. I would not marry Arthur either. I was not going to resume my role as the Princess of Riche.

What life I had lived in the past few days, woke me to more than the handsome Ravenfae Prince of my childhood fantasies. It had woken me to what I wanted, and it was none of those things.

There was time to decide.

Once my spirit form merged back with my body, I'd have time to escape that life and figure out how to move on and do it without Korven.

I couldn't be in his life, and though I didn't know the reasons, I would respect him for not promising what he couldn't uphold.

He'd never really leave me anyway. Like the ink across my back, I'd hold these memories of us together always, thankful for every one. But I couldn't leave him to his life without something of me to hold onto, too.

I wiped away more berry juice from my skin and wrote my own note after slipping back into my billowy dress and Korven's cloak.

Be back soon. Punishment to be delivered.

—YS

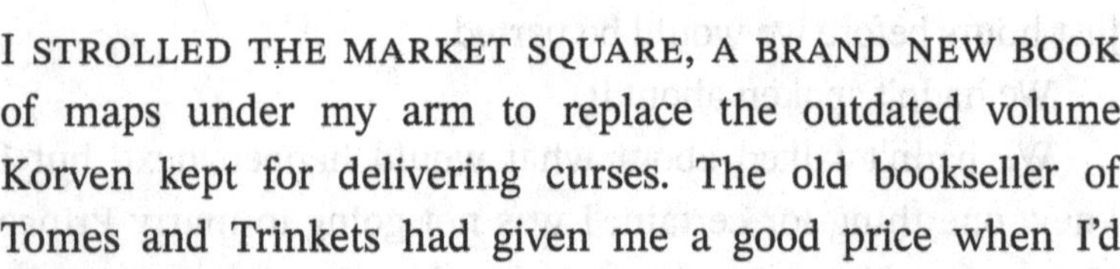

I STROLLED THE MARKET SQUARE, A BRAND NEW BOOK of maps under my arm to replace the outdated volume Korven kept for delivering curses. The old bookseller of Tomes and Trinkets had given me a good price when I'd explained the book was meant as a gift for the man who had helped end my curse.

I hurried back towards the Rose and Briar, hoping to intercept him from wherever he'd gone when a flash of black feathered wings at the top of a bell tower caught my eye.

I rushed inside the altar hall, avoiding the attention of priests lighting candles and incense in tribute to the Goddesses of the Veil.

The pews were packed with people on the night of the Cursed Moon. Those who feared receiving a curse sought solace, murmuring their prayers to the Goddesses of the Veil.

Mothers did what they could to keep their new babes in their bellies to avoid the curse at birth.

I hadn't been so lucky.

I slipped in the back door that led to the tower stairs, hoping to surprise Korven. We could watch the sun set over Havenshire and make our way to the castle and be done with this death curse on us both.

I took the steps a few at a time, my heart racing by the time I reached the top of the landing, slipping through the door and stepping around the copper bell.

"Hello, darling girl," came a voice rich and feminine. "I was hoping we'd meet."

I gasped as she turned my way. Almost as tall as Korven, her face was sharper with a small mouth and hooded eyes in an earthy brown. Black ink traced across her lids in a wide sharp line to the sides of her face, reminding me of a bird of prey. Her raven black hair was piled elegantly atop her head, weaving through her dark crown with long curls framing her face. A hint of silver glinted at the tips of her black feathered wings.

Korven's mother was terrifyingly beautiful.

Her dark gown trailed the stone as she advanced my way with a smirk. "It is almost time, is it not?" she purred.

"Until the moon is-is full, high in the sky. We have a little time yet," I managed, still catching my breath.

The Ravenfae Goddess stopped, a deep-gutting laugh escaping her. "*We?* Oh, my. What has my son been up to?"

I swallowed my fear. "Have you not heard? Fiola paused the curse, giving me,"—I gestured to my head, still translucent—"this spirit form and just ten days to find the one who can love me most. He must kiss the lips of my body in the castle. She pulled Korven into this task as well." I paused, considering how angry she would be hearing the last part. "He...is bound to the same fate as me if we fail."

Reshina's eyes sparked and her brow raised as she stepped closer, her slender shoes clicking on the stone. "Seraphine," she cooed, lifting her hand to squeeze my shoulder. "Sweet, sweet child, Korven has never and will never be bound by another Goddess's magic. It is his birthright as a child of the Veil. This curse is yours. *You* are the sole casualty."

I released a breath. "But Fiola said—"

"She said what would give you hope and the help you needed. She and Korven have always known he would not die by this curse. It is yours, and yours alone to bear." She hummed, tilting her head, her wings curling behind her. "My son cares for you. Or he would have left you to your fate."

"He knew?"

"Yes. Does that change you?" She narrowed her eyes, studying me. "Ah, I see. You've let your heart give in to fantasy. You've dressed up the Ravenfae Prince as the hero to save you."

She stepped back, giving me space to breathe. "What will you do now, I wonder? What will you do with the time left for you in this world, Princess of Riche? The night is coming and your time reveals an end you cannot escape. What will you do with the last hours you've been given before the moon is full and your fate is sealed?"

Her words damned me.

Like the curse made for me that night of my birth under a moon-drenched sky, my fate would be known to all in such precious little time. Would I live or die?

Korven had deceived me, but he had decided to stay, unbound to any conditions Fiola gave.

But why would he pretend? Why would he care when we had just reunited and he didn't know anything about me?

"My son soars to meet me here. Stay and say your piece or go and do what you will with the last hours given to you. Your heart is yours, Seraphine, and yours alone."

I saw his shadow as a black line in the sky, headed straight towards us. I turned abruptly, bolting through the doorway and down the stairs with her last words ringing through my head.

Korven

IN ONE GREAT SWOOP, I LANDED IN FRONT OF MY mother. "What is it?" I stormed. "I'm busy tonight."

She laughed, folding her arms at her chest. "What you are is late. I called for you an hour ago."

"I had...appointments to keep."

"With her?"

"Some. Why have you summoned me?"

"Courtesy."

"Courtesy?" I growled. "For what?"

"I do not mean to hurt you, Korven."

"Tell me, Mother."

"Your sister is betrothed."

The blood drained from my face. I knew because I felt it pooled in my heart, bleeding from my failure.

She settled herself on the stone ledge. "It was her choice, my dear."

"She's fifteen. She doesn't know what she's choosing or the consequence of her—"

"You don't give her enough credit. You've always

protected her so fiercely. I wonder, was it to protect her or because you needed someone to protect?"

"You wouldn't understand my need to protect Morella."

She paused. "No, perhaps I wouldn't."

"She's fucking *fifteen*. Can't you at least see that's far too young to make that choice?"

She shrugged. "I was younger when I was shipped away to produce heirs."

"I need to speak to her."

"And you will," she replied in irritating ease. "But you know what she'll do. She'll dig her feet in further. Her future as my heir was something you would not allow and now you would deny her this? A choice?"

"Are you considering naming me your heir instead?" I asked, stunned.

"More than that. I'm offering it to you." She stood, the Curse-bringer ring in her hand, open for me to take. "You've done well these past five years, and you've proven yourself capable."

"And what of the matriarchal line?"

"I imagine you will pass this ring to a daughter of your own one day. It's stipulated in our contract, bound to the ring."

This was what I wanted.

This was what I'd been working for, but Morella...she didn't need to decide this now. I needed to see her.

"Who is her betrothed?"

"A faraway king, as they usually are. She does not leave for some years yet. You'll have plenty of time to try to convince her otherwise. As for your current duties..."

I nodded, swiping the ring from her hand. It morphed and folded into a dark band of obsidian shaped like a feather. I slipped it on my thumb.

It was done.

I was the Cursebringer, just as I had set out to be years ago, saving my sister from the heavy weight of this fate. I'd deliver the curses of the land just as my mother had for hundreds of years.

"I need to be somewhere," I muttered, dismissing myself from our conversation. "You have the names ready for tonight's curses under this moon?"

She waved a hand dismissively. "I'll take care of this night. You don't start until the next Cursed Moon. I made sure it would be so."

I swore under my breath. My mother had been unable to love me my entire life, but it was these little motions, these boons she would occasionally dole out that made me wonder if she wasn't constantly struggling against the rules of her own curse.

"Thank you," I said softly. "I will return to Brackish Castle before the next moon."

Her dark red lips sparked into a smile. "And will you return alone?"

My body shuddered and I looked to the sun, setting clearly in the golden sky. I had less than an hour before the glow would leave the horizon and Seraphine and I would make our way to the castle. I reached for the pouch of gold marks in my pocket, knowing I'd need to be quick in my last stop.

"I have to go," I replied, refusing her an answer.

I didn't know if I'd return alone.

I hoped not.

I leapt from the ledge, headed to the market square.

"Till we meet again, my son," she called, her words following me through the evening air.

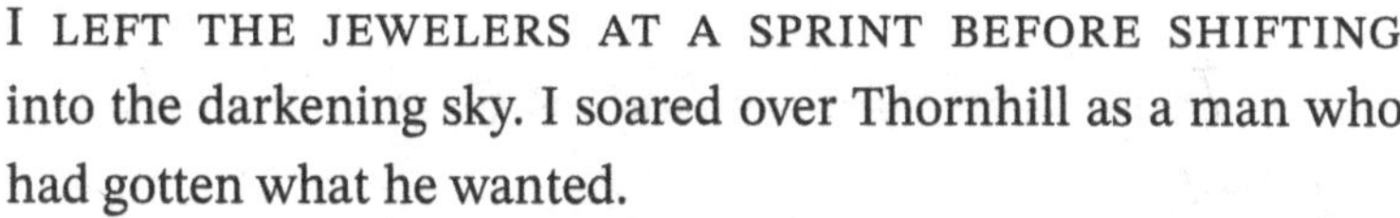

I LEFT THE JEWELERS AT A SPRINT BEFORE SHIFTING into the darkening sky. I soared over Thornhill as a man who had gotten what he wanted.

And still, I wanted more.

My heart felt light, free...afraid.

The coward in me had bought two pieces of jewelry.

One, a necklace with a pendant shaped into a sycamore leaf. I had plans to imbue it with magic and Seraphine could call me to her side if ever she rubbed its surface.

The second...the second was a ring. The single stone was a raw cut amethyst set above a simple gold band. I had noticed it in a shop window while we'd searched for her dress.

I'd inquired about it when I'd stopped at the market for food a few days later, and now, as I shifted back, I felt the weight of it in my pocket.

I feared her answer if I asked her.

If Arthur broke the spell, would she consider him to be her future?

Fuck, I hated that duke.

If he couldn't save her tonight, I could.

Maybe I could all along.

"Phinie," I whispered harshly in the darkened room of the Rose and Briar, searching for her form on the bed. It was cold and empty.

Her dress gone, her shoes gone, my cloak...gone. And on the small table in the room, next to the last of the smashed bramble berries, lay the note I had written to her upon my departure. She had left an open book with a dot circled on a map of Moonstone Wood.

A line was scratched out on the parchment as if she'd written something before she wrote,

> *This is where you can find me if you ever need a friend.*
>
> *Thank you for staying when you did not need to.*
> *—YS*

YS...Your Seraphine.

And next to her carefully crafted words, which raked a knife through my chest, was the most perfect stained kiss of bramble berry juice.

Seraphine had lips.

CHAPTER 26

Seraphine

S NEAKING INTO THE CASTLE WAS DIFFICULT.

If I had been just an earthly spirit, I'd have managed so much easier, but as it was, a good hour before the moon was full in the darkening sky, I was mostly solid. I reached up to touch my nose and beyond while hidden in yet another alcove, waiting for the servants to continue on their way and stop gossiping about the duke who had just arrived at the front door to the palace.

Arthur was here.

But I didn't need him.

I slipped out of the shadows as the servants left, sticking to the tapestries along the wall, silent in my bare feet and soundless dress. I had ditched my shoes at the back door of the castle kitchens, solid enough to pretend to be a servant myself, my head bent and no one to really care to glance my way after I'd grabbed a large pitcher of wine to carry.

If anything, the servants were dressed quite lovely and whispers told me it was in celebration of Prince Urik's betrothed soon waking from her curse with a kiss.

Many of the whispers included that it was not the Prince of Havenshire who could wake her, but a Duke of Riche.

But it wouldn't be either of them.

No duke, no prince.

Just a hidden princess, determined to set her own fate.

I had lips.

I loved me.

And I knew in my heart, this was what Fiola wanted me to learn all along.

I would never leave, or have to decide whether I was good enough company to stay.

I loved me most.

And in the days of my curse, I had finally learned that curse-breaking lesson.

Every inch of my body that had returned was not from the duke or the man I loved. It was all from me—loving me, taking care of me, protecting and advocating for *me*.

My decision to wake myself from the curse had brought lips. My run through the winding paths to the back door of the castle had brought me a nose.

And as I ascended the winding stair of the tallest tower, avoiding the two guards at the bottom landing who gossiped to a few servants by the door, I felt my cheeks form, burning with exertion as I climbed and climbed, the pads of my feet lightly tapping along the dusty steps of the tallest tower.

I came to the door of the tower room, breathless, a smile as wide as the wingspan of the prince I wished had asked me to stay. The latch clicked and I pushed through the door, closing it softly behind me—ready to face my body and return to it as a woman uncursed, and loved.

Urik had placed my body upon an ornate four poster bed with white sheets and white drapery hanging in silvery swaths of translucent fabric that flowed gently with the breeze coming from the open window. Seven alcoves around the circular room hosted seven tapestries depicting the human kingdoms of Revelry.

I approached, steadily studying myself outside of myself.

I looked so fragile—a weak creature waiting to be saved. My skin was cold, my heartbeat so slow, I would have assumed my death would be sooner than the time I had left for the Cursed Moon's rise.

"It's alright," I whispered, brushing back my golden curls, fanned across the downy pillow. "I love you most."

I closed my eyes and leaned down, placing a soft kiss on my own lips.

I blinked once. Then twice, straightening myself upright next to my body. My eyes stung with the chilled air and the wind picked up, blowing sharply through the room. I touched my face. I had eyes. I had a forehead, long flowing hair, and a tiara I wanted to toss out the window.

I had returned.

But not to the body on the bed. That body went cold. I checked for a pulse and found none.

I'd done it. I'd returned, but to this body that had formed from my spirit.

Voices sounded on the stairwell and I recognized the rage of Urik's fury.

Jolting from the bed and scrambling behind the tapestry of Riche, I peeked from the small alcove to see Urik shoving Arthur through the tower door, sword to his back.

The duke was bruised, battered, and all together unwell, hunched and struggling, as blood pooled at the corner of his lip.

"Do it and be done," Urik spat. "Then I can send you back to that castle where you can rot, just like your mother."

I flinched at his cruelty, transfixed as Arthur turned in a

rage, facing Urik's sword at his chest. He pointed at my dead body. "She will never love you," he seethed. "She will never be yours. The day I made that deal with you is a day I'll regret for the rest of my life."

Urik chuckled darkly, piercing Arthur's skin with his blade. "Your life may be over soon enough anyway. Do it. Break the curse."

Arthur turned, approaching the bed.

My heart raced so loudly, I feared they'd hear it and find me hidden, placing me back into the prison of princess I had just escaped.

He sat on the side of the bed, pulling at his jacket to wipe the blood from his mouth. In a light whisper he said, "I'm so sorry, Seraphine. So, so sorry."

"Get on with it!" Urik yelled.

Arthur brushed my body's cold cheek, bent his head and kissed my lips.

"Well?" Urik snarled, pushing him back.

Arthur stumbled from the bed, his face crestfallen.

A sound of disbelief at my situation escaped me, and I slapped my hand over my mouth but not before Arthur caught my eyes behind the tapestry, cold shock across his face.

"Why isn't she waking?" Urik kissed my cold body, then rose, shaking it desperately. "Wake! I command you to wake!"

Arthur's face calmed as realization hit him. One slight nod was his assurance to me that he would keep silent.

"Wake, damn you!" A slap hit my dead body's face, the only hint of color rising from the force of Urik's hand.

"Enough!" Arthur shouted, sprinting to grab the Prince of Havenshire. He didn't quite make it to Urik before a stream of black shot through the window, pummeling my betrothed to the ground.

"THAT WAS THE LAST THING YOU'LL EVER DO," I growled through clenched teeth, the blade of my knife already deep in Urik's chest. His blood pooled over my hand as I pushed deeper, reveling in the visage of fear on the bastard's face.

I had arrived at the open window, my lungs bruised from how far I'd pushed myself to get to her—to save her—and this fucker not only defiled her with his lips, he had the death wish of slapping her cheek, something he should have known he would not survive.

I rose, wiping his blood along his embroidered vest, once gold, now stained crimson as he gurgled pathetically in his last moments of life.

"Prince Korven—"

"Shut the fuck up!" I shouted, another knife lifted from my boot, pointed at the duke. I took one glance at the rising moon and rushed to Seraphine's side, taking her cold, lifeless hand in mine as I kissed her lips.

She didn't have time left for me to apologize or confess

how fucking much I loved her, so I just kissed her instead, my body shaking, begging her to wake.

She didn't stir.

She didn't lovingly blink those violet eyes and smile up at me.

No, she remained a lifeless beauty.

Her red cheek faded, her chest unmoving, but at peace as if she slumbered softly in the top tower room of Castle Havenshire.

"*Seraphine*," my voice broke and I kissed her again, my face hot as tears fell on her skin, sliding down her cheeks and onto the pillow.

"No! *Please!*" I cried, lifting her body and pulling her to my chest as I shattered, stroking her hair, kissing her again and again with no sign of life left in the woman I loved.

"Korven!" The duke was behind me, shaking my shoulder. I set her back on the bed and turned in a rage-filled grief, my knife at his throat, shoving him against the stone windowsill, ready to toss him out.

"You said you'd do it!" I screamed. "You said you'd break her curse!"

I pushed him further, my tears and broken heart blinding me.

He grabbed the knife at his throat with one hand, fingers digging into my shirt with the other. "I...didn't...need...to!" he managed.

"Stop, Korven."

The most beautiful voice filtered through me and I whipped around, almost knocking the duke out of the window before he caught himself on my wings.

I didn't care.

I couldn't fucking care because there she was, standing in

the middle of the room as her body lay dead, blanketed in a white wedding gown.

A cry of relief struck my chest, and I fell to my knees, my knife tumbling to the floor as she neared, barefoot, her gown of pale lilac and blush billowing around her like some Goddess yet unnamed.

"Seraphine," I breathed and she smiled with lips so lovely and pink.

She came to me, settling over my lap, nestling herself into my arms so warm and alive and fucking perfect.

She wiped at my face, kissing away my tears.

"How?" I stumbled. "Who?"

"I broke the curse. I didn't need anyone to do it for me."

I swallowed hard, touching her, feeling her, assuring myself she was real and solid and here with me. "You said *goodbye*," I choked, pulling the book of maps from my jacket. My voice broke again, "*This is how you said goodbye!*"

A wave of sorrow crossed her face, and I pledged right then to never see it again. She used her sweet lips to kiss my forehead, taking my face in her hands. "You never told me I didn't need to."

A huff of a laugh escaped me, and I shook my head, sweeping a hand across her face—solid, and so beautiful. My thumb brushed her mouth and she kissed it, a smile breaking across her bramble berry lips.

"Then I'm a fucking *idiot*," I growled, pulling her in, pressing my lips to hers. She sighed, giving into me fully, our lips melding, caressing, my tongue meeting hers, my breath matching hers, my heart beating with hers—my woken Seraphine solid and mine to love.

ONE YEAR LATER

Morning light filtered across Seraphine's face through the diamond paned window, casting a rainbow of pastel hues along her cheek.

"Phinie, my love," I whispered in her ear.

She groaned and yawned, turning in our bed, wrapping her arms around me and snuggling into my neck.

I slipped my hand under her silky nightgown and brushed my fingers along her tattooed spine. That always worked.

She groaned again, stretching her legs to tangle with mine and mumbling against my skin, "Why do you wake me, Ravenfae Prince?"

"The Cursed Moon is tonight. I have a lot to prepare and the morning is all I can give you." I kissed her hair, breathing in her scent of dried herbs and fresh dew she collected for her tinctures.

"There's more than the morning you can give me, Prince," she cooed, pressing herself to my cock.

"You're insatiable," I laughed.

"Kettle, meet pot."

I chuckled into her hair. "I have something for you. It's

been a year. One year I've gotten to hold you every night and wake with you every morning."

Her head snapped to mine and she blinked blearily. "Is that all? It feels like it's been a lifetime."

I agreed. From the moment I carried her in my arms out the window of that tower, we'd been mostly inseparable. I'd brought her home to the cottage in Moonstone Wood and the world believed her dead. The story went that her curse remained unbroken and the Prince of Havenshire took his own life in the tragedy of his betrothed never returning to him—a story told and fueled by none other than the Duke of Riche. Or King of Heartstone Castle, I should say.

Fuck that duke. He was still an asshole.

"It's been one year and before I make love to you at least twice, I have a few gifts."

She snorted into my neck and I raised her chin to steal a kiss.

"You brought me gifts?" she said dreamily.

I stroked a thumb under her bottom lip. "Raven, remember?"

I slid the package from underneath my pillow, pulling her up with me and placing it in her hands. I'd taken great care to wrap it neatly in rose stained parchment, a pink peony fresh and bound in twine over the wrapping.

She brought the flower to her nose. "It's beautiful. Where did you find one that bloomed so early in the season?"

"I know a gardener who owed me a favor."

She eyed me with a knowing grin and set the flower on the small chest of drawers at the foot of our bed. She unbound the twine and carefully unwrapped the package, gasping and holding up blush colored stockings. She laughed in glee, "I love them! They're beautiful, Korven!"

She shimmied out of her worn stockings, long overdue for

her lover to knit her new ones, and pulled them up her legs. She hopped out of bed and spun in a circle. "How do they look?"

My eyes wide in disbelief that she was fucking mine, I nodded, a raspy, *good*, coming from my chest. I leaned forward and pulled her back to bed, handing her the other part of her gift. She settled in, folding her legs underneath her and carefully opened the black box.

A sound of shock left her as she gently picked up the book bound in black cloth and opened to the first page. "Cursed Goddess of the Veil?" she whispered, gently flipping through the brittle pages.

"The first copy ever penned. By my mother herself."

"Korven...this is incredible."

I slid my fingers up her leg, taking her hand and kissing the ring that had been there almost an entire year. "My mother was glad to be rid of it. I told her you'd be its keeper if she ever wants it back."

Seraphine shook her head. "I will. I will keep it and cherish it. Thank you."

She closed the book gently, adding it to the chest next to the flower she didn't yet know would never stop blooming. She wrapped her arms around my neck, settling herself over my lap as I leaned against the stone wall.

"I do love you," she said, kissing my chin, my cheek, my brow. "My husband, my lover, my Prince."

I slid my hand behind her neck, slipping my fingers through her golden hair, one hand lifting her nightgown to cup her ass grinding on my cock.

"Be mine forever," she whispered, adjusting her entrance over me, pulling a growl from my throat. "Love me most."

I settled her hips over mine as she began to move so

sweetly. I brushed my mouth across hers, lifting her body and setting her down beneath me, thrusting deep, just as she wanted. I lived in her cry of pleasure, sealing my kiss with my promise. "Done."

no meaning. Available on Kindle Unlimited and major booksellers.

If you enjoyed this book, (or any book!) I'd like to encourage you to rate/review it. Algorithms from sites like Amazon, Goodreads, and Barnes & Noble base their recommendations of books from a book's number of reviews and ratings. These reviews and ratings are especially important to indie authors like me who do not have high budgets or marketing resources to gain a large readership. We depend on people like you to help us, so thank you for your support. Happy reading!

Acknowledgments

When I set out to write my next book after finishing *A Blightress of Wrath*, I struggled to understand where in the hell I was supposed to go after leaving the world of Felgren Forest.

Fairytales have always been stories I've loved to read because of their short nature and romanticism, so a stand-alone retelling felt like the right place to land.

I am so thankful to my readers (that's you!) for your encouragement, support, and general heartfelt comments, messages, texts, and reviews of my work. If I didn't have you, this passion of mine would feel far less useful, so thank you so very much for reading, reviewing, and sharing my stories.

Rachel, sometimes I think about that first message of yours when you were dubbed "eagle eye" and just what life has been like with you since then. Yes, friends can be soulmates, and wow, are we lucky to have found each other. I love and squeeze you to pieces.

Desiree, you are so fun, funny, and freaking brilliant. I know that if we lived just down the street, we'd be bugging each other constantly and probably get nothing done. Thank you for being so excited about what I write and being such an amazing friend. Let's do another buddy read, like, it's time, girl.

Elaina, I am so thankful to have you to reach out to. Anytime I'm weary of my actual skills and possible future, you seem to know, and text to remind me that you believe in me. I believe in you, too, and can't wait to see what comes from you next.

To my family and friends, thank you for your words of support and encouragement as I keep trekking on in this author life.

For my three loves at home, I think we have a good routine now with my writing. Will, I'm sorry mama writes bad words sometimes in books and that you occasionally catch a glimpse and scold me. Violet, yes, I did write a book about a princess, but you can't read it for quite some time, Little Love. Reed, yes, I did offer this book to your mother to read, but I think she'll be alright.

Chelsey Ann Tompkins was born to be a storyteller, specializing in tales of magic and swoon-worthy romance. Her adolescence was spent reading countless historical romance novels and classic literature, leading to a love of brooding men and strong-willed female characters. When she is not dreaming up heartbreaking romance stories, you can find her brewing yet another vanilla latte, at the library with her kids, or reading while indulging in the blissful silence a bubble bath provides. She resides near Seattle with her husband and two children.

instagram.com/chelseyanntompkins
tiktok.com/@chelseyanntompkins
threads.net/@chelseyanntompkins